MONTANA REPORT ON BIGFOOT

BOOKS SIX OF THE DRC FILES

KEVIN A DAVIS

MONTANA REPORT ON BIGFOOT

CONTENTS

INTRODUCTION

It's about time I slipped Jade into a story, beyond an awkward phone call. Kristen gets awkward in person!

A little camping and relaxation may be what she needs, but you know I can't leave it at that.

A couple visitors from a previous book are brought into the mix since we're over on the west side of the US. A small mention in this book is the seed for the Phoenix DRC series with Zach Graves.

I hope you enjoy

Atlanta's Guide to Cryptids: Book One of the DRC Files is a 2024 Gold Medal winner of the Florida Authors and Publishers Association President's Book Award in Adult Fiction: Fantasy/Occult

ALSO BY KEVIN A DAVIS

If you'd like to be kept up to date on this series or my other books, please head to my website and join my mailing list

The DRC Files - an episodic paranormal procedural with Kristen Winters and team out of Atlanta

The Phoenix DRC - a spinoff of the award-winning DRC Files where Zach Graves joins the team headquartered in Phoenix, Arizona

The Khimmer Chronicles - the spunky Ahnjii makes new friends and enemies while stranded on a cryptic-filled earth

The Sorrowborn Trilogy - a YA Adventure Romance by April Davis & Kevin A Davis featuring the indomitable Caitlyn

The AngelSong Series - Haddie deals with ancestral powers in this gritty series of angels, demons, and fallen angels

Website KevinArthurDavis.com

Facebook @KevinArthurDavis

KevinADavis on Instagram

KevinADavisUF on Twitter

CHAPTER

ONE

Pete Wright walked behind his mentor, Russell Howard, along a chilly forest trail heavy with the scent of pine. Owls called around them in an ominous warning while a cluster of coyotes laughed somewhere to the south. Through a thin canopy, the full moon lit the two men's solemn march with shafts of bright light.

"If this works, Johnson will be our first target?" Pete asked. The mayor had stolen the election, and something needed to be done about it. Otherwise, he never would have agreed to anything as dangerous as what Russell had proposed.

Russell's balding head shone in the moonlight with his remaining graying hair appearing like half a glowing halo, though his nature leaned far from sainthood. "He will be our test. The writing promised that we'll be able to control him with the demon's words. If that is the case, he might cast down half the council before he dies at his own hand." No emotion embellished the man's tone, but he never displayed any beyond occasional outbursts of rage.

Pete swallowed and pinched at his mustache. "After

dealing with the council?" He left his secondary interest in the plan unstated.

"Your philandering wife and her newest harlot will follow soon enough. Perhaps a suicide pact would be the most appropriate. Our foremost concern is the well-being of the city and rooting out these socialist worms that eat away at the fabric of our nation. I will let nothing stand in the way." Russell didn't turn around completely, but his glasses glinted in the moonlight.

If the ritual worked as described, then little could stop them, if they avoided notice. Practitioners of their arts knew well enough to avoid the attention of the Consociation and the dragons' minions. Pete shifted the satchel he carried on his shoulder and zipped his jacket higher against the cold.

Ahead, Russell's abandoned family mine lay like the entrance to a tomb with gray timbers supporting a rusted pair of doors. Over a hundred years prior, it had yielded a smattering of gold, enough to finance the family's purchase of ninety acres of wooded vale.

Russell dug under his jacket for the key and slipped it into the heavy padlock that clasped the doors together. As the lock clicked, the coyotes cackled and yipped.

As Pete followed Russell inside, he shivered, questioning his resolve once again. The air stunk of foul water hidden deeper in the shadowed interior. He twitched when the electric lantern snapped on and illuminated the chipped and cracked walls of the tunnel. Old beams of weathered wood braced the sides and ceiling every ten or twelve feet, but they'd never given him any sense of safety. His nostrils flared as he drew the heavy doors closed and slid the metal bar down to lock them in.

With confident steps, Russell marched onward without lowering his head like Pete did. After they passed the third support, the blocky altar ahead showed only as black against shadows, except where gray bones caught the lantern light. Built eighty years ago of ashen remains, it showed the signs of wear on its six-foot long top.

"The corporax first," instructed Russell. He stepped to an alcove at the side to set the lantern on a shelf next to a pair of older kerosene ones. Light and shadows danced upon the myriad of objects, bottles, jars, and boxes stored there. Hints of sharp herbs, kerosene, and fouler mixtures hung in the stagnant air.

With a wince at his aging joints, Pete dropped the satchel against the wall and crouched beside it. The square of linen lay folded at the top, and he rose, shaking it out. "Center?"

"Correct." Russell gathered a tray of squat, black candles already well used. He placed it on the edge and returned to his alcove.

Upon the linen, Russel had painstakingly drawn a sigil of Baphomet in black ink, with semi-circles of sigils at the points of the pentagram filled with the goat's horns and beard. Pete laid out the cloth with care, knowing it would be adjusted.

"Bring the rest here." Russell worked in a brass basin, placing elements of the ritual on the bottom.

From the satchel, Pete brought out three Ziplocs; one with fresh yarrow flowers, the next dull gray graveyard dirt, and last, the corpse of a kitten, starved to death before it could suckle. The ritual's final ingredients had been most timely, harvested in the past two days. He placed them within Russell's reach, then stepped back, watching his mentor work.

The practitioner arts had been part of the Howard family's heritage, contributing to their wealth and position. Pete had stumbled into the knowledge as Russell's college roommate in the mid-'80s. His skills lacked in direct proportion to the number of grimoires and spell books he'd collected compared to Russell's library.

As expected, Russell adjusted the corporax before placing the candles upon the linen, in line with the points of the pentagram, and lighting them. The brass basin followed, decorated with ingredients as artfully as a chef's special and placed over the center of the Baphomet sigil. With the silver athame and pewter chalice in position at each end of the altar, they stripped off their jackets and shirts in the frigid cold of the mine. The ritual had been specific, if not odd.

Pete's toes curled against the rock, but he kept his fists to his side instead of wrapping his arms about himself in a feeble attempt at warmth.

On the other side of the altar, Russell showed no reaction to the temperature as he brought the athame to his left arm, poised over the chalice. "Of my sacrifice, blood to thy lips." He cut a three-inch stripe from close to his elbow and bled against the pewter edge. "By mine life, will, and word, I bind you."

Shivers shook Pete from the cold, not the ritual. They had performed dozens with success, though none as formidable as this one. Russell had been thorough. At worst, they would summon nothing.

When Russell dropped the bloody athame to the altar top, it rattled, and dark droplets soaked into the black composite. He ignored the blood still leaking down his arm as he poured the contents of the chalice into the bowl with careful spirals. Thinned by the alcohol already in the cup, the bright red liquid lifted bobbing yarrow flowers.

"I command Faerzien to rise from Tarus and submit to my blooded binding." Russell's voice held the authority to master even a creature from Tarus. He lit the sandalwood splinter in a black candle and tossed the flame into the bowl.

With a whoosh, the contents ignited, and Russell repeated his intonation, demanding that a demon from Tarus serve their needs.

Pete watched the altar with eagerness. If the ritual worked, they would right the imbalance in the city council. His treasonous wife would meet a well-deserved end. Between these two outcomes, he would restore his finances. There might even be new opportunities available.

The stench from the burning basin intensified, the black smoke billowed heavier than expected across the ceiling to roll down the side walls, and Russell grimaced in the middle of his chant.

Pete almost spoke, interrupting the ritual. His confidence wavered.

Smoke exploded.

The light from the candles and lantern snuffed out, leaving Pete in pure darkness.

Russell gurgled, almost laughing. Then he rasped.

With a trembling foot, Pete took a step backward. Something had gone wrong.

A groan escaped from Russell before it morphed into a throaty, inhuman growl.

Pete spun and ran for the exit. His shoulder scraped rock, but that set his feet in the correct direction.

The brass basin crashed to the floor along with lesser sounds of the chalice and athame clattering. Nails sounded against stone.

With a brutal slam of his forehead, Pete found the double doors out of the mine. He staggered, but his hand slapped at the latch, seeking a grip to free it. Numb with cold, his finger found a familiar edge and yanked it.

The digging nails ripped against the rock, gaining on him.

As the latch released, whatever Russell had become slammed against him. Together, they burst through the doors and spilled into the bright moonlight.

Claws ripped into Pete's arm, and his hips screamed as he slapped onto the freezing trail. He slid to his back, scraping thin skin.

Straddled over Pete, the creature coated in short fur could only be a werewolf. Somehow, Russell had touched the realm of Ya Keya, not Tarus.

Ears had grown to points, and the mouth and jaw to a muzzle. Thick claws kneaded into Pete's chest, shredding flesh and scraping against ribs.

Unable to process the pain, Pete froze at the edge of consciousness. He watched in horror at the sharp white teeth of the werewolf as it opened its mouth wide. When the cryptid twisted its head down to chew into the side of his stomach, Pete passed out.

TWO

I trudged through the small airport, juggling my go bag on my left shoulder, repurposed to its original backpack usage. My purse strapped across my body, I held a Luna roller in my right hand, and my cell pinned to my shoulder with ear and earrings. "I just landed."

Coffee aroma in the warm air caused my head to swivel, adding a threat to my precarious balancing act. A bored attendant scrolled their phone beside a case of Danish and bagels, but at this time of the afternoon, I doubted the offerings would be worth appending a cup of old coffee and a stale lunch to my present load.

"Like, still in the plane, or are you in your rental car?" Jade asked. In the background, I could hear a laughing conversation and a dog barking. "Well, we're going swimming. You have Meghan's dad's number. Be safe. I love you. See you soon." My daughter sounded happier than she had in a long while.

I paused to relish her mood with a cheeky smile, and before I could respond, she hung up. My backpack slid off my shoulder with a jolt into the crook of my elbow, jostling my phone loose. To further amuse two men who sat doom-scrolling on a bench, I dropped my roller bag and used my knee to soften the cell's fall. Never skilled at hacky sack, I launched the device two yards ahead of me.

"Crap." With a shrug, I hoisted the backpack to my shoulder and jogged after my phone, leaving the Luna face down on the floor.

A hairline crack in my screen protector marked the bottom right corner. The cell woke quickly enough, but I'd be replacing the protector when I got back home. I ordered them by the pair.

The day had proved as long as I'd expected, with an early flight out of Atlanta and a delay with the connection to Montana. Jade, her friend Meghan, and the girl's parents were already at the Swan Lake campground. With sunset hours away, I planned to set up my tent in daylight.

After a wait of forty minutes to get a blue Subaru WRX with a scent of stale fries, reminiscent of my car during my college years, I wound my way through the city, surrounded by the beautiful mountains of Montana. Dark clouds moved in as KZMN played classic rock, and a flash of rain unleashed as I turned south, forcing me to turn up the volume.

"So much for swimming," I said to myself.

As quick as it started, the rain stopped, leaving wet roads and sparkling trees. The truck ahead kicked up mist, so I kept fiddling with the squeaking wipers to find the balance between a dry squeegee and too much water. Eastern mountains rolled down to the asphalt, ending in abrupt embankments at the road's edge.

The trees on the right disappeared, exposing a dark Swan Lake to my right. No one parked at the little tourist lookout that jutted out onto the shore. Had it been sunny, I might have been tempted. In a minute, the wood returned with the occasional house or business, though the gas station appeared dark and closed.

The spray off the highway lasted until I could pull into the campground and search for Birch Loop. I craned my neck to read the little signs. Tall trees backed site eleven with some newer growth and surrounding grass. Damp leaves stuck to the wet asphalt drive.

A big man with a gray beard and dark hair sprawled in a camp chair under the canopy of a fifth wheel. He held a can of beer until I pulled into the drive, then he deposited it into the holder of his chair and popped up. With a genial smile, he couldn't help but guide me in with gestures like I was a Boeing 747. A missing vehicle to tow his RV confirmed that Jade, Meghan, and the mom were off swimming, despite the weather.

"Hey, um, Kristen, I'm Harry." Mr. Turner stood over six feet, and stooped when I opened my door. "Jade's out with the girls swimming. I can give you directions if you want to join them."

The temperature had dropped from the rain, and I shivered, stepping out. "They still swimming, you think?"

Harry glanced at the wet ground and trees, as if just noticing it. "Uh, maybe not."

"Yeah, they'd get wet." I winced.

His brow creased. "Uh."

I wasn't about to drag out my bags until there was some place to put them. "Jade said you had a tent?"

"Yeah." He hustled toward the RV. "Should have pulled that out."

"Probably good you didn't."

With a confused expression, he paused at a latch on the side of the fifth wheel. "Why?"

"The rain."

"Oh, yeah. Not to worry about that. Done for the

weekend. Going to be hot on Sunday. 80s." He dragged out a tarp and marched around to the section of wet grass.

By the time we set up the tent, with little help on my part, a smiling woman pulled a black Ford truck into the drive. Small hands waved from the back seat, but I couldn't parse Jade from Meghan until they exited. Heart skipping, I finished tossing my pack inside, and strode toward them.

Jade's black hair had grown out to her shoulders, and she'd gained two inches since I'd seen her last. Her slight frame and tan skin tone spoke of her father, not my side of the family. "Mom," she called, running to me.

I hugged her, careful not to cry. We'd had a lot of ups and downs since I'd moved to Atlanta. "I've missed you so much. I love you."

"I love you, Mom."

Mrs. Turner, Cheryl according to our emails, offered a warm smile as she lugged bags out of the truck. Short and curvy, she appeared small compared to her husband. Meghan stood as tall as her mom, with pale brown hair plastered to her head, cut short just below her ears.

"How was swimming?" I asked Jade.

She snorted. "It rained, but you know that. Do you like the campsite? It's almost like we're alone out here."

The trees blocked any view except for the road. Jade did better around fewer people. "It's beautiful."

"Harry didn't offer you anything to drink." Cheryl made the statement a jest to cause him to wince, rather than a question for me. "Beer, wine, pop, water?"

I was thirsty, and released Jade, though she let me keep my arm around her shoulders. "Pop is fine."

Jade's dad had enjoyed camping, and we always had a pot of coffee brewed. The Turners hadn't started a fire, so I took it off the potential menu. I could sneak out for some later.

After a tour of the park that included a walk down to the shore of Swan Lake, a respectable dinner of Cheryl's grilled cheeseburgers, and an arrangement of air mattresses to my daughter's approval, I offered to drive Jade to a convenience store fifteen minutes north. Her expression told me I'd be going solo.

"Can Meghan and I hang out in the tent?"

I shrugged. "Sure. Need anything?"

She shook her head, wagging her whole body, then giggled as Meghan darted for our tent. I waved to the Turners, who had bundled up to sip their drinks by the fire.

The temperature would be chilly overnight, but Cheryl had prepared for us with sleeping bags and extra blankets to top the air mattresses. She'd insisted that I didn't need to bring anything but clothes and toiletries. For me, that meant plenty of sweatshirts, sweatpants, some jeans, two pairs of shorts, T-shirts, three different jackets, and enough underwear to last a week.

Since I tended to be a klutz, especially around food and nature, I'd probably go through everything in two days.

I pulled out of the campground with the sun deep in the west and eastern clouds already tinged with color. Along the highway, Swan Lake opened up on my left for a section, offering a calming sight with a few boats getting in their last hour. Like much of the mountains, roads butted against rocky inclines where trees and brush found impossible footholds.

At a curve, I passed a convenience store with gas that appeared closed and hadn't even popped up on my search. It had that local feel of "when we're open, we're open." I kept following my map.

When I pulled up to the gas station, I hoped that the "Welcome Fishermen" sign meant that the store offered more than bait, then smiled at the "Hot Pizza" banner.

Two cars parked out front, and an SUV at a gas pump, so the store hadn't closed early. Purse over my shoulder, I stomped through the chilly weather to the door.

Inside, the heat had me loosening my jacket while I searched for coffee. I'd grown up around places like this with bobbers and hooks on one aisle and cups of noodles on the next. The nostalgia, along with camping with my daughter, brought out a warm sense of contentment, tinged with the knowledge that I'd eventually leave for Atlanta and my job at the DRC.

Holding a huge bag of beef jerky, a familiar-looking woman with red hair cut in a pixie watched me wander toward her in my search. "Kristen?" she asked. "Kristen Winters?"

THREE

I stepped closer to the woman, trying to place her in my memory. "Yes." The scent of pizza that hung in our corner of the store distracted me. Then I remembered the werewolf from Mika's team. "Wait, Dagen?"

She smiled, offering a single nod, before her expression tightened. "Did Pyre send you out here?" With her black windbreaker zipped up, I hadn't noticed the white collared shirt she wore underneath, and just noted the black slacks she wore with polished shoes you wouldn't see in this rural store.

She's on a case. "Mika's here? Is the entire team here?" I blinked, then composed myself and answered her question. "No, I'm camping with my daughter."

"Camping." Dagen studied me for a moment. "We should talk." She strode for the front counter.

As she paid for her snacks, I leaned toward the young man at the counter. "Any coffee?"

"Wouldn't call it that, this close to closing. Help yourself to a cup, no charge." He pointed me in the right direction.

Dagen called out behind me. "We'll be outside."

I forced a smile and nodded over my shoulder. *If I get dragged into something, Jade will never forgive me.*

Even with abundant cream and sugar, the coffee lived up to the employee's promise. I winced a smile as I said my thanks and stepped outside.

Dagen leaned in the driver's window of the SUV parked at the pumps. With windows tinted and in the late hour, I couldn't make out anyone else. *Mika, Dagen, Phistrel, and Olivia.* After meeting them, I'd intended to research them on the database, but had forgotten.

The wind gusted, and I tugged at my jacket as I walked to Dagen. She stepped aside as I approached, exposing Phistrel with a decent start to a beard joining his mustache. He offered a terse greeting of, "Hey," before pointing to the passenger side of the Ford.

As I veered around Dagen and the front of the vehicle, the sight of a delicate man with black hair who sat in the passenger seat caused me to stumble. He wore wire-rimmed spectacles and a dark suit. Olivia, petite and pale with sharp eyes, sat in the back. I licked the spilled coffee off my fingers, cringing at the bitterness. *Who is this?* Dagen hadn't answered my question about Mika, but their team was here. Despite the cold, the window was rolled down.

"Um, Kristen Winters, out of Atlanta."

The man smirked and chuckled, the expression and high cheekbones growing familiar. "I'm Mika. Pleasure to meet you, Kristen Winters."

I blinked as their voice and demeanor clicked into place. Mika had presented as nonbinary the last time we met and seemed to enjoy my surprise now. My cheeks flushed as I spoke. "I didn't recognize you, sorry." The coffee tasted worse as I took a sip to cover my fluster.

Dagen snorted. "They enjoy it."

Mika rocked their head. "When in Montana, do as the heteros do." They waved off the comment, resting an elbow out the window. "Here with the kid?"

"And her friend and family. Should I be concerned?"

"Bear burritos," snickered Dagen.

"Probably. We've got what we believe is a rogue werewolf," Mika said.

With a raised eyebrow, Dagen studied us from across the hood. "I think newly turned, from the details. It's hard to rein in emotions at first, and if you're the wrong temperament in the first place, it can become blind rage. Start off as a jerk, end a jerk."

"Could be a personal grudge," said Phistrel from the driver's seat. "A Biera would have been here for a new turning. Neddie sent word out; none are in the area."

I recognized the term "Biera" from my research as the group of werewolves who supported a witch when they traded their abilities for the power of Ya Keya. "Who's Neddie?"

"She works operations," answered Mika. "I imagine you assume drugged?"

Without a glance at Dagen, who likely knew of my case while still a lead detective in Grand Junction, I shrugged. "I've had experience with that." Werewolves could become addicted and violent. "However, I don't know the situation."

Mika held my eyes, then tilted their head so the lights over the gas pumps caught the purple sheen of their black hair. "Care to take a look with us?"

Jade. To delay my response, I took a sip. I groaned and threw the coffee in a nearby garbage bin. My smarter half considered heading back to the campsite and whisking Jade away from whatever mess had brought Mika and their team out to Montana. "Sure," I said.

Olivia popped open the back door, as if she'd been waiting for a signal. "Water?" she asked.

I ambled between the door and pumps, my purse snagging on the hose. "Please." As I slid inside, she handed me a bottle.

Phistrel did not drive like Marie; if anything, he moved with such care that I asked the question I should have before getting in the vehicle. "How far away is it?"

He glanced at his cell on the console. "Nine to ten minutes."

We drove toward the mountains to the east, where the sky had turned gray. Olivia smelled of the same paste David used to protect his skin in daylight. In my previous life, before the DRC, I didn't expect to be around vampires or werewolves. They existed, but at such low percentages that a witch would only meet a handful of them combined over a lifetime. As familiar as mountains and bait shops had felt half an hour ago, cryptids were my new normal.

Mika twisted in the front seat to face me. "Victim is Paul Bates, a witch. Death occurred forty hours ago, at approximately two in the morning. He lived alone. Owned a successful real estate agency with eleven employees. The police are not investigating what they consider a bear attack."

"A witch?" I asked.

"Neddie confirmed," added Olivia. "Does that change anything?"

I frowned. "I don't know." We drove into a wooded section, dark with shadows. "Why did it take two days to pick up the case?"

Still turned back to face me, Mika smiled. "Took a

while for local police to load their photos. How often do bears eat people?"

Not just kill, but eat. "It's rare. Food would be plentiful this time of year. Maybe in the middle of winter, but not the beginning of June."

Dagen snorted. "A newly turned werewolf wouldn't have any natural skills at hunting in any weather. The initial hunger can be debilitating. Think Scooby Doo with roid rage."

I kept my expression deadpan, suppressing a grimace. "Anything else to indicate a werewolf versus a bear?" Locals would be on the lookout for the latter.

"Claw marks," said Mika. "The initial pictures didn't have proper measurements, so we had to wait for the coroner to send us their findings. It would be a small bear."

Olivia spoke, watching my reaction. "Damage to the door is inconsistent with a bear. It targeted the latch side, smashing through there." She paused, eyes intent on mine. "The few examples of forced entry by bears showed the predominant pressure at the top."

Forced entry by bear. How would she even find that data? "If it is a newly turned werewolf, what kind of escalation or de-escalation should we expect?" I spoke to Mika, hoping Dagen would have insight.

Dagen leaned up, peering at Olivia. "Unfettered, a lone werewolf will kill to feed as needed. Without a mentor, they'll remain more feral than human. Ever wander around naked in the woods?"

"Bearly." I raised my hand to my face at Olivia's sharp, focused gaze. "Not wander, no."

"Itchy and scratchy. Mosquitoes. Believe me, you'd keep the fur coat on."

I offered a tepid smile. The powers Ya Keya offered held no interest for me. Why would anyone want to be a werewolf? Witches chose the option on rare occasions, but the reasoning had always eluded me.

Mika wore a slight smile, watching me. "Any thoughts?"

A snort erupted from Dagen. "You know I'm right. Newly turned."

"Open-minded." Mika's words sound tired, like an often-stated reminder.

Her arm pressed to the back of Phistrel's chair, Dagen grinned and leaned toward Mika. "I'm right, and you know it."

"Statistically, not that often," said Olivia in a calm, matter-of-fact tone.

Dagen slumped into her seat, rapping at the window. "Stuff your statistics."

"Dagen, we have company," Mika crooned with some measure of enjoyment.

"Bite me." Dagen leaned up, eyeing me. "Not you."

As we turned along a curve, Phistrel turned on his high beams, lighting a three-story house on a slope with pines and mountains as a backdrop. A porch circled the second floor. Raw wood and green roofing gave the log cabin a natural feel.

A white sheriff's SUV sat in the drive leading to a garage.

Mika had turned to the front, so I glanced at Olivia to see if she'd expected local law enforcement.

Her sharp eyes searched the scene in front of us. "Neddie called them in."

Rocks formed a decorative border on the slope between us and the house. A concrete wall housed a garden around stairs leading to the second floor. Yellow tape and plywood covered the front door.

As we approached, a woman exited the vehicle bundled in a thick coat and wearing a broad-brimmed hat. She had an affable smile as she motioned Phistrel to park beside her vehicle, and as he pulled in, she walked alongside his driver's door.

He rolled down his window, letting in a biting chill.

"Almighty," the officer exclaimed as she peered in at us. "A whole truckload of Feds. For a bear attack?" Loose brown curls dangled as she grinned and rested against the door.

With a casual demeanor, Mika leaned forward. "We end up on the strangest assignments, you wouldn't believe. I'm Special Agent Mika."

"Deputy Rebekah. Is Mika a Russian name?"

"Ukrainian." Mika opened their door, so I did the same.

Under the DRC, my interactions with local enforcement had been mixed, but Rebekah seemed pleasant enough, despite her observations or opinion of federal agents. I forced a smile onto my face and shivered against the chill.

Olivia slid out behind me, eyes flicking into the woods until I had to turn and search the darkness myself.

With everyone dressed in slacks and proper shoes, I felt a bit out of place in my casual camping attire. *Not supposed to be on a case*, I reminded myself.

The two of us rounded the vehicle as Mika shook the woman's hand, then pointed to the covered door. "Mind if we take a look?"

Rebekah shrugged, digging into her pocket. "Knock yourself out. Bring bear spray?" She chuckled. "Just kidding." Keys jingled, and she tossed them to Mika. "Side door on the porch. Lock up and leave them on the woodpile in the back. I'll collect them tomorrow."

Dagen had exited the Ford, her nostrils flaring as she stood by Rebekah.

I waited behind Mika as the deputy pulled down the drive. From Dagen's expression, I guessed she'd smelled something. "What is it, Dagen?" I asked.

"Werewolf," she said, taking the keys from Mika. "It's a couple of days old, but distinct. Give me a sec."

Lovely. As Dagen started to the front door, I pulled out my phone to let Jade know I would be a little late returning.

I texted Jade, starting with a grimacing emoji. The hairline crack in the screen protector annoyed me.

RAN INTO SOME PEOPLE. I'LL EXPLAIN LATER. EVERYTHING GOOD AT THE SITE?

It took a minute before she responded.

WHO?

PEOPLE I KNOW FROM WORK.

DID YOU PLAN THIS?

NO. OF COURSE NOT.

Red-headed Dagen disappeared along the porch, while Phistrel and Mika leaned against the Ford and Olivia studied the entrance to the house. I stared at my screen, waiting to see if Jade intended to reply, or if we were done. When I frowned, lips twisting, and pocketed my cell, Olivia studied me.

Mika straightened and walked away from the SUV. "So, camping? What, like hiking and all that?"

"Yeah, they've got a hike planned." I'd skimmed through a lot of the details that both Jade and Cheryl had elaborated through texts and emails. Another thin layer of guilt spread across what my text to Jade had started. "Tomorrow, maybe?"

"You're just here for your kid." Mika smiled.

A light turned on in the house, drawing all of our attention. With quick spry steps, Olivia moved to a window and peered inside. Did she speak so little because she focused on her observation? I'd gotten used to David's cavalier mannerisms, and assumed they were a vampire default. Those I'd met in New Orleans had seemed entitled and arrogant.

Phistrel walked to the porch with Mika following, so I fell in behind, stuffing my hands in my pockets. As we passed the first set of windows, light from deeper in the house hinted at rich wood, carpets, and stone. The ground sloped away as we turned the corner to the side facing northwest.

Dagen poked her head out of an open door. "Were-wolf for sure. Male. It might have slept here after feeding."

As Mika and Phistrel entered, Olivia hung at the doorway, inspecting the glass doors.

"These would have been easier than the front door," I said.

Olivia raised her eyebrows, as if agreeing. "Front door would have been visible from the southwest, or quicker than walking around the porch."

I turned toward the southwest. "So, maybe coming from the direction of Bigfork." With a slow spin, I considered the expanse of wild forest to the north, then the incline up to the mountains. "No reason to assume they touched Ya Keya in the wilderness; they could have been in their living room. If they are newly turned."

Olivia cocked her head, locked eyes with me for a moment, then darted inside toward Dagen's voice.

"Here, at the stairs. They haven't cleaned up the blood." Dagen pointed to the steps leading upstairs.

The sharp scent of old blood hung thick despite the open door. Heavy leather couches sat in a sitting area with a stone fireplace to my right, with equestrian decorations and a painting depicting three horses.

Phistrel and Mika clustered beside Dagen, where a staircase rose from the front entry area, turned at a blood-splattered landing, and rose overhead to the third floor. Underneath, more stairs led to the dark floor below.

The rustic log cabin walls and ceiling beams blended with finer bronze statues and rich rugs that suggested afflu-ence. "Did he have an alarm?"

I walked to the edge of the stairs, heading down. Dark stains dripped from the back side of open steps to the top level, leaving no doubt where Paul Bates had died.

Mika answered my question. "Wasn't set. Maybe only used it when he left."

A statue of a rearing horse stood on a decorative table beside the railing to the stairs. It appeared undisturbed, but one of the small pictures next to it lay flat, near the edge. Smaller figurines remained upright.

Dagen climbed the stairs to the upper floor, stepping through the dried blood on the landing. Between the wall splatter and drips on the stairs, I didn't need to see the crime scene photos to guess the extent of damage that the body had endured.

A door beside the stone fireplace led into a smaller sitting area. I turned on the light but didn't see any evidence that it had been disturbed.

The entry to the ruined front door had blood smears on the pale tile from the werewolf leaving. Wheeled tracks of a gurney cut through the blood. Overall, the scene had been contaminated with traffic from the locals.

It wasn't until I followed Phistrel into the kitchen that I found an oddity. With care, I picked my path over obvious bloody footprints on the tile to an uncorked bottle of red wine that sat on a granite counter.

Mika entered, finding me peering at it. "Empty?" she asked.

"About halfway."

Phistrel grunted from where he peered out a glass door. "Let's hope our victim was drunk when the werewolf got him."

I leaned in to study the label. "Is that blood?"

"You think the werewolf stopped for a glass of wine after its meal?" Mika came closer, tilting their head at the bottle. "It might be." They pulled out their phone, took a photo, and sent it to someone, typing for a minute.

Olivia had joined us at some point and stood motionless at the edge of the kitchen with her eyes flicking from the bottle to me. "Why did it come in here, then go back out the way it came?" She pointed to the glass door at the back. "Wouldn't even have to break it; just unlock it."

Mika spoke while typing. "I've asked Neddie to send Everek. I want this scene detailed."

My mind still churned at the idea of an addled werewolf drinking wine. "How much control do we think this werewolf has?" It disrupted my belief that it might be a drug-induced killing since my experience had been with a very rage-filled, chaotic cryptid.

"Not much," answered Dagen as she rounded the corner. "Don't have any scent of him upstairs or downstairs, but he was in this room."

I pointed to the wine bottle.

Dagen snorted. "Not sure how well that would pair."

Olivia shared my cringe. "I'm walking the perimeter."

"I'll go with you," I said, then wondered if she'd mind that.

She headed down the stairs to the bottom floor, where Dagen had turned on the lights. "You're not convinced it is a newly turned werewolf?" Olivia asked.

One step held the splatter from the dripping off the landing, and I avoided it. "I don't know enough to have an opinion. Dagen would have the best experience, or at least some anecdotal support. I trust that there's been a werewolf attack, and that something consumed some of the victim's flesh."

We headed for the door to the northwest, unlocking it and exiting. The night air had plummeted in temperature, and the stars had taken the sky like a sparkling blanket.

She stopped outside and faced me. "Some predator or scavenger could have entered through the open door, before the body was found."

I shrugged. "The scene is pretty trampled. Maybe the original photos might show something."

She scoffed and headed to the right, with her focus on the building. "They only took pictures of the body. At least, that's all they uploaded. I'll mention to Mika that we might want to check with their photographer as some only supply relevant images."

My phone dinged with a message, and I stumbled on the uneven ground. Jade had sent a text.

Sleeping with Meghan in camper.

I didn't blame her, and with a rogue werewolf about, I'd prefer she was inside rather than alone in the tent. Several responses went through my head, but I kept it simple.

Sorry.

We walked up the incline to the back corner, where the kitchen light shone out of the window. The rest of Mika's team leaned against counters and talked, noting us as we passed.

Jade didn't text again, so I pocketed the cell. Coyotes yipped and cried to the south of us, bringing my attention to the sloped woods so close to the house. I shrugged off a chill. The market had been a ten-mile drive. "How far do you suppose we are from the Swan Lake campground?"

"Eight miles. You should pack up. At least get into a hotel or something." Olivia had an unsettling way of tracking my thoughts just from my expression or words.

I'd considered the idea and knew that Jade would hate it. A tent offered no protection at all.

As we reached the corner of the garage, in sight of the team's SUV, Olivia stopped me with raised fingers. She never turned to face me, but lowered the hand to point downslope ahead, past the drive and road.

I drew in a sharp breath and held it, but found only dark shadows and a star-filled horizon. My eyes flicked to the woods closer to me, then back to where she'd gestured. Nothing. Motionless, I waited for something to show itself, or for her to explain.

We stood there a full minute until voices sounded from the other side of the house. A boisterous comment from Dagen echoed, then a quieter reply came from Mika.

"Did you see that?" Olivia asked.

"No. What?"

"Eyes. The light must have caught them, because they were red, then just glinted."

"Where?" I leaned forward, squinting. A chill tickled my neck.

"Forty yards straight ahead in the woods." She broke into a march across the drive, heading for the entrance at the road.

After a pause, I followed with a glance toward the front

of the house where the others were walking along the porch. David's reckless behavior had seemed a personal trait, but perhaps vampires just had little concern about their personal safety. On any other occasion, I would have had my gun.

"Right behind you." I pinched into the mossy-green of Dur-Alf and prepared a shield.

Mika and the group hushed their conversation, and footsteps padded on the wooden porch.

Dagen reached us first with barely any sound except her breathing. "What?"

I remained silent, trailing behind both of them now. Nothing moved in the woods except a faint breeze sweeping through branches.

"I saw red eyes," Olivia said. "Something."

Mika strode up beside me. "Kristen?"

With a quick glance at her, I shook my head. "I didn't see it."

Her chin lifting, Dagen's nostrils flared as she sniffed the air. She growled under her breath, then her jaw muscles tightened and rippled to shift her face. The stronger lines and slight elongation toward a muzzle came with a darkening of her fiery hair and matched the deeper tone of her voice. "Werewolf."

Their steps quickened, and I hustled to keep up as Phistrel passed me with a long stride.

Dagen took the lead, with Olivia at her shoulder. We crossed the road, and I considered tossing a detection spell from Haven, but this wasn't my team.

My stomach fluttered as Dagen crouched. The shadows in the woods cloaked all but the closest trunks, leaving an impenetrable depth where anything could hide. She would be the first to know if we encountered a werewolf.

Mika whispered without turning around, "Phistrel."

With both of his hands, he pinched out the soft fluffy white of Haven and tossed detection spells into the depths ahead. Small animals lit up as bright spots of white. Birds hid in treetops, rabbits clustered to our left, and rodents scurried away. Nothing large showed, not even a raccoon.

"Dagen?" Mika asked.

"He was here. The scent is faint and there's a trace of something. It's — confusing." Dagen continued forward, growing slower with each step. "I should have an obvious trail."

Branches tugged at my pants and coat, and the soft layer of detritus sank beneath my steps. I smelled pine and earth, but nothing else. With the others in the front, I veered around unseen obstacles and avoided a fungus-covered log.

I plowed into Phistrel's back when Dagen stopped.

"It's everywhere, like it ran about spreading its scent," she said.

It didn't sound like the mindless werewolf, intent only on feeding, that she'd described earlier. "Does that change things?" I asked.

"Yeah," Mika said. "We're staying in the house tonight. If it wants to play hide and seek, I'm all for it. I don't think we should traipse any deeper in the middle of the night."

I grimaced, wishing I'd driven my rental. Jade would not appreciate me showing up in the morning. At least the werewolf wasn't ranging anywhere near the campground.

"I'll drive Kristen back." Olivia's voice to my left surprised me. I hadn't heard her move in the darkness. Vampires couldn't read minds, but I wondered about her.

With a frustrated snort, Dagen's face relaxed, and she spoke to me. "Better let your boss know what you've been up to."

When Mika rested their hand on my shoulder, I jumped. "She's right. Pyre will want an update." With a gentle nudge, she motioned me to follow Olivia, who already trekked toward the dull lights of the victim's house.

My feet caught in the clutter of the forest floor while I imagined Pyre's response to all this, and my involvement. Would she be displeased? *Not as much as Jade.*

FIVE

Once I climbed into the passenger side of the team's Ford Escape, I called Pyre, assuming she'd be in her office, but with the time difference, perhaps asleep. The hairline crack clicked under one of my fingernails.

She didn't answer, and I wasn't sure I wanted her to. If I'd ever called her this late when we weren't on a case, I didn't remember. I texted her.

I met up with Mika's team in Montana. Went to a crime scene with them. Will call tomorrow.

Olivia drove with as much care as Phistrel had. Maybe my trips with Pyre just eased the experience by comparison. She waited until I dropped my phone in my lap before speaking. "The bottle. The point of access. The surveillance."

My eyebrows raised, surprised by her summation of points that bothered me about the scene. "A single picture knocked flat."

Her head cocked, but she didn't take her eyes off the road. "Picture?"

"On the table by the staircase. There's a large bronze rearing horse, other statues, another picture, but that picture was knocked down."

"Picture of?" she asked.

"A young man."

"I'll get Neddie to find out who that is." Her voice relaxed, as if dismissing the concern.

"Could have been knocked down by the locals, but the table's thin and the statues seemed more likely to fall with a bump. Maybe they did, and they put them back straight, missing the frame." Any list of circumstances could have occurred, but I'd learned to note everything.

"The bottle," she continued.

"Beyond Dagen's joke, she never mentioned whether the wine fit her theory of newly turned werewolf." The wine didn't fit the idea of an addicted cryptid either.

"What does the wine fit; connected to the departure through the front entrance?"

The heat from the vents offered a pleasurable warmth to my fingers and face. I appreciated Olivia's methodical breakdown of the information. "Well, the blood on the label suggests that it was touched after the killing, at least, and most likely after the — consumption of the flesh."

"Whereas, the wine in between killing and feasting would fit the same access and entry best."

I agreed, and that concept disturbed me, as did her choice of words. "So not a very frenzied feeding if he took a break for a drink."

"The entry point would indicate he came from the woods where I saw the eyes. Any other direction offered easier access." Olivia moved to the next point, as if we'd exhausted discussion on the first.

"Agree." I had no argument since we'd just gone

barreling into those woods and Dagen had confirmed the presence of a werewolf.

"The surveillance. Red eyes."

My forehead wrinkled with a frown. "Have you ever heard of a werewolf, transmogrified or not, having red eyes?"

"I'm counting it as a trick of light. If Dagen hadn't picked up the scent, I might have considered other cryptids. Why watch the house?"

"I don't know why he would. Dagen's voracious, newly turned werewolf doesn't fit sitting outside for a couple days."

"He didn't attack Rebekah." Olivia turned onto another back road with only the headlights to pierce the darkness. "Any other predator would have left the area in search of food, or attacked the deputy. Instead, it hung at the edge and studied us."

"Maybe it scented Dagen," I suggested.

"Plausible." She pulled onto a highway with faded painted lines and no streetlights. A truck passed, heading south. "What's your assessment of these unusual aspects?"

"I don't have one. Without information from Dagen, it would be difficult to form opinions. Does Mika often sleep at the crime scene?"

"No, we're bait."

I'd suspected Mika's intent. "If it were that irrational, wouldn't it have attacked when we charged into the woods?"

Olivia's lips flickered with what might have been a smile. "That's my appraisal, but Mika's tricks sometimes work." She gestured to my lap. "No response from Pyre?"

I flipped my cell over. "No. I should message Finn." The content of the text was similar, alerting him that I would call Pyre in the morning.

Surprisingly, he answered immediately.

Just landed in Lake City. We've got a case. Twelve dead at a bar with outdoor music. Pyre's talking with Mika now. Where are you?

My lips parted. *Why didn't they call me?* Finn must have gone with them, and that would upset his husband, Gary.

Do you need me to head back?

Not yet. Pyre will decide. She says to take some time with your daughter and she'll call in the morning.

Okay. Gary?

I'll make it up to him. He was angry when I left, but I checked in when we landed, and he understands.

Stay safe, that's what he cares about.

It would be late there, maybe midnight. Finn and Pyre's pups wouldn't be getting much sleep. Another layer of guilt spread across what I'd built up over Jade.

Finn ended the conversation with an emoji.

"They've got a case," I told Olivia.

"You headed back?"

"Not yet. I'll talk with Pyre in the morning." I relaxed my grip on my phone, fighting the worry over the possibility of having to leave in the middle of Jade's trip. She'd never forgive it.

In silence, we drove over a narrow bridge with the closed gas station ahead. In the warmth of the vehicle, I'd grown thirsty, but could wait until I returned. Would Jade come out or stay in the Turners' camper?

Olivia pulled up on the driver's side of my rental. "I enjoyed your insight. Good luck with your daughter."

"Thanks." I almost replied that I'd see Olivia tomorrow, but I didn't know if that would be the case. In truth, I couldn't be sure why Mika had invited me to the scene. "Good working with you."

"Same."

I stepped out into the cold, closed the door, and hurried to open the Subaru. The heat took a while to warm up as I drove back, and my focus shifted to Jade again. We'd planned this trip for weeks, and I was ruining it for her. She needed a mom in her life.

When I pulled into the campground, dogs barked at my arrival. Some campers were sitting by fires, talking and laughing. Other sites were dark, or at least quiet, some with a light lit above their RV door.

The windows of the Turners' fifth wheel had a bluish glow, flickering as if from a movie. My headlights pierced the dark woods behind as I pulled in and shut off the car. Thirsty, I bundled up and exited, heading straight for a large cooler by the picnic table. Cheryl had made sure we had soda and water available.

The recognizable sound of light sabers echoed from inside as I unlatched the cooler and dipped my hand in freezing water and ice for a bottle. I took two, not wanting to repeat the process any time soon. Before I had the first cap off, I had to pee. *Damn.*

Jade opened the camper door dressed in blue pajamas and an unzipped windbreaker. A ship whined in the background from the movie. She waited to speak until she'd stepped down and closed the door. "What's going on?"

"Aren't you cold?" I asked.

She tucked her windbreaker tighter and crossed her arms, pinning it there. Her head cocked as she waited for me to answer.

How much could I tell her? We'd always danced around my work at the DRC, but I'd let enough slip that she knew I didn't have a position at the FBI. "There's — something out there that killed a man two days ago."

"And you're the only one who can do something about it? Did you know before you came out here?"

"I didn't know. I met some people who I knew from a previous case."

"While you were out getting coffee?" Her accusing tone made it clear she did not believe me.

"I've never lied to you. Hid things from you, and still do, but what I say is the truth." I drank some of the water and offered her the other bottle, but she refused.

"So there was a murder. You met some people you know and started chatting about it — for hours?"

"We were hunting — searching for the killer. I went to the scene. I'd rather you sleep inside the camper tonight."

Her tense expression loosened as her eyebrows dropped. "What is it?"

I drew in a deep breath, then lowered my voice. "We are pretty sure it is a werewolf."

Jade pulled back her head in surprise. "They aren't really dangerous. That's just folklore, myth, and Hollywood."

"Generally, yes." I'd never fully detailed my experience with the Grand Junction police and been the one to impress on her that werewolves weren't a threat. "This case is different. Can you stay inside tonight?"

My layered guilt thickened as I realized that part of me manipulated her by emphasizing the risk. I already believed that it had positioned itself outside the victim's house. The werewolf, whatever its purpose or condition, hadn't ravaged the eight miles between the campground and the crime scene.

With a glance to the side, I amended my request. "Out of an abundance of caution. Maybe no hiking in the mountains."

Her eyes widened. "No hiking? You know we have a hike planned tomorrow."

I hadn't remembered the exact day. "The police are searching for a bear, so there should be news about it. Just delay it, until my friends can catch him." After being in Jade's sights after going with Mika's crew, I'd just about eased her out of it, then fanned the flames again over the hike.

Her arms had dropped to ball her fists, and her jacket flapped open in the cold. "You're ruining everything. Why do you have to do this?"

"I'm warning you because I don't want anyone hurt."

"I wish you'd never come."

My heart dropped. "I understand that." After I'd moved to Grand Junction, our relationship was strained, and it had just gotten worse. "I want to be here with you. I'm sorry things haven't turned out the way we wanted."

Jade glared for a moment, then spun to head back inside. As she opened the door, blasters fired from the movie.

"I have to pee," I said.

SIX

Groggy, I started in the dark to Marie's call. "Hello?"

"I woke you. Sorry."

My eyes wouldn't focus enough to read the time, so I pulled my sleeping bag over my head and laid the phone near my chin. "I'm awake. You heard about the werewolf." I made the statement more for my foggy brain than Marie.

"Yes. Mika said you were helpful. We'd like you to check in with the team this morning."

Jade would disown me. "I'll call. I got Mika's number."

"I know I'm interrupting your vacation, but it's important. Mika believes you'll add a different bias to their investigation."

"Should I take that as a compliment?"

"Take it however you want. Mika requested your help."

If I hadn't come out camping, my relationship with my daughter might have fared better, but I didn't want a man-eating werewolf lurking about her. "Okay. I'll check in with Mika when the sun comes up." I winced at the not too subtle hint.

"I appreciate it."

"Oh, how's your case?"

"Going nowhere. It has the same markers as the rave cold case. Lots of witnesses, but no leads. We're still interviewing."

"You were up all night?" I asked.

"Not the first time. Check in with Finn when you have an update." Marie hung up.

The sleeping bag smelled like laundry detergent. Outside, even the woods were quiet with no morning birds or people stirring. I'd have to deal with Jade. If Mika's team didn't catch the werewolf, someone else would end up hurt. At my brief mention of a bear killing a local, Harry had been happy to tell me they had repellent. I should check with Dagen to see if that might work. Either way, I didn't want my daughter going on the hike. We'd have time to discuss it in the morning.

When I awoke for the second time, the sun had lightened the sky enough for me to see inside the tent. What might have been an entire flock of birds chorused in the woods, a dog barked somewhere in the campground, and Cheryl suggested the eggs were done well enough to mortar bricks.

I plucked my phone out of my armpit at a couple minutes after 7 a.m. with two messages from Mika waiting. They'd be there after I hit the bathroom. As I moved a leg to sit, the air mattress tilted me onto the tent floor with all the grace of a baby giraffe.

"Mom's up," Jade said. Her voice had none of the venom of the night before.

With my sweatshirt zipped and slip-ons flopping, I stumbled out into a chilly, cloudy day. "Good morning."

"Uh, that cooking aroma wake you up?" Harry's

cheery stammering speech wasn't something I'd look forward to each morning; not before coffee.

"Yeah." I forced a smile.

"Bathroom's all yours," said Cheryl. "Coffee's in the pot by the stove. Help yourself. It's all yours, we don't drink it."

Depending on the size of the pot, that should work. "Thanks."

I paused on my way to plunder creamer from the fridge and found sugar packets by the mug beside the coffeepot. With a warm and entirely consumable beverage, I proceeded to take a seat and check my messages from Mika. Their first had been an offer for breakfast at 6 a.m. with a link to some restaurant. The second caught my attention.

SHERIFF REPORTED ANIMAL DISTURBANCE NEAR PROPERTIES ALONG RED OWL TRAIL. WE'RE HEADING THERE.

Mika had texted five minutes ago, probably waking me up. Without too much thought, I replied.

I'LL CATCH UP. WILL CALL FROM CAR.

Sometime overnight, I'd come to the decision that a man-eating werewolf posed more of a threat than Jade's ire, barely. When I stepped out of the camper with my coffee, my daughter smiled, and I nearly lost my nerve.

"Um, eggs and bacon." Harry pointed to a plate beside Cheryl. "There's muffins and butter, too."

"Sounds great. Is it going to rain?" I asked, hoping the weather might cancel the hike, rather than an overprotective mom.

"Wasn't supposed to. Between that and the bear, we're postponing hiking until tomorrow. Swimming and town is a better bet." Cheryl spoke, gesturing in directions with her fork.

Jade watched my reaction, not giving any tell in her

expression. *Is the chance of rain why she's not as upset?* I reached for a blueberry muffin and butter. "Probably best."

"Bring a suit?" Cheryl asked.

I focused on slicing cold butter and spreading it on the fluffy muffin without making too much of a mess. "Did. However, I've got some officers in the area who asked for my feedback on one of their cases. It shouldn't take long."

Jade sagged, and my heart followed. *I'm sorry, honey.* Like glaze on a roast, I smeared on another valid layer of guilt.

"Ah, bear hunting," joked Henry.

Cheryl gave him a bland glare, as if she could tell the undercurrent between Jade and me. "Well, check in when you're done, and we'll let you know where we are. Sorry you got tangled up in work."

Meghan teased Jade about the cold water, as if trying to clear the mood. They left their plates half-finished when they ran inside under the premise of getting changed, though Cheryl reminded them it would be a couple hours before they'd brave the chilly lake. I finished what I could of the meal and stood to make my exit.

With a light touch on my arm, Cheryl caught my eye. "Try to get with us today. Jade needs this."

My throat too thick, I nodded without a reply. I changed into jeans and a fresh sweatshirt, wishing I'd had time for a shower, and climbed in the fast-food scented rental to find Mika. I'd tucked my large travel purse in the trunk with my extra clothes, content with just my phone, keys, and wallet in my pockets.

Google led me past the convenience store where I'd met Dagen, then onto a gravel road that threatened to lead all the way back south to the campground before cutting west. Any reservations I had about helping find this werewolf faded as I placed it closer to where we had spent the night.

Fifteen minutes later, I pulled up behind Mika's Ford parked at the side of the street and climbed out. A short driveway led around a corner ahead of them. Dagen stood at the front bumper, sniffing the air. Clouds softened the sky up to the mountains in the west. The scent of past rain mixed with pine.

"We've got him in the area." Mika rested against the SUV with Olivia, gesturing in a vague circle. Their hair was still glossy black, and if they'd changed clothes, it was a similar suit.

As I approached, Phistrel exited the driver's side. "Ready?" he asked Mika.

"Let's go bother the locals." Mika strode toward the drive, and I followed with a double-step.

"What were the reports?" I asked.

"Dogs and horses upset. A woman we talked to said she saw someone walking across a field east of here last night. She called the sheriff first."

Dagen jogged up to join us. "It's our werewolf. But I swear there's a second one." She frowned at her latter statement. "Makes no sense."

My step faltered in the grass. "Wait. Two?"

She rolled her eyes at Mika. "Forget to mention that in your message?"

Mika cocked her head back and forth, not replying.

With a side step, Dagen studied her leader. "Do you think I'm just making it up?"

"Not at all. You said yourself that you weren't sure."

One werewolf fit Dagen's theory, ignoring some irregularities I'd discussed with Olivia, but two didn't sound right. Either Dagen had got the scent wrong, or we were dealing with something else. "Assuming there are two, what would be the scenario where one of them would kill and eat a human?" I held my finger up to delay them from answering. "What if a rational, responsible werewolf attempted to track down and stop the newly turned one?"

"I like that," said Mika.

We turned onto the drive that cut through pines with an easy curve to the north. Buildings nestled a good bit down the slope, and I wondered why we hadn't driven instead of walked. The back of a brown truck faced us, but nobody moved outside. A "no trespassing" sign tilted ahead.

Dagen snorted. "Could explain it."

When we'd walked halfway to the houses, a dog barked in the woods to our right. Birds lifted into the air, sweeping south. Head cocked, Mika stopped.

A shrill yelp came from the dog. No one paused. We all sprinted into a run.

SEVEN

Before we crossed the grass and hit the forest, I struggled to keep up. Dagen and Olivia had already crashed through the underbrush out of sight as the dog yipped in short, fearful bursts.

The ground sunk half an inch at each stride, moist from rain. Early summer growth hid all but the tree trunks stretching up to the sun-speckled canopy. From its cries, the dog moved away, and as we careened through the woods, I questioned our reckless approach.

A vocal click sounded ahead, and I promptly ran into Mika's back. I stumbled to the side, flailing at brush to steady myself.

Mika caught my elbow and pulled me upright.

Birds chided from the sky above, but the surrounding silence tightened my chest. Haven flashed through the bushes to the left, and Phistrel sent two detection spells into the trees. The team lit up with Dagen and Olivia crouched ten yards ahead.

With my arm still grasped, Mika nudged us forward,

taking careful steps. I cringed as leaves crunched underfoot, but Phistrel walked no quieter.

Dagen waited to speak until we crept up to her. "He's out here. Scent is fresh."

Olivia had her Glock in hand while scanning the surrounding area with short, clipped turns of her head. "Just the one?"

With a brisk nod to confirm, Dagen led the way. Mika and Phistrel had weapons drawn, and I might have felt vulnerable, but I relied on my quick magic. In caution, I readied a shield spell from Dur-Alf.

Mika drew from the Mer realm, then faded from my sight, leaving only a disconcerting Haven ghost of them beside me that distorted the woods. Our combined footsteps crunched through the underbrush that left little doubt of our approach, like we were the bait for this werewolf. I did not trust enough to keep my eyes focused in just the direction Dagen led us. My muscles tensed, as if I might run, and my heart fluttered. Olivia's quick head movements increased; perhaps she too, felt the impending threat. Dagen's features shifted so that her jaw grew more pronounced.

Phistrel drew two new detection spells and tossed them yards ahead.

A large thud crashed behind us.

I bit off a cry and tossed my shield behind myself and Mika. A werewolf covered with thin, dark brown fur hit the invisible barrier. Without hesitation, it raked claws into the surface and catapulted overhead toward Dagen and Olivia.

My fingers already pinched Dur-Alf at both sides, digging a shield and a binding. I fought a panic unlike any I'd experienced during my time with Marie's team.

Olivia shrieked, not in pain, but rage. Her sudden,

violent movements reminded me of the rogue vampires we'd fought.

The werewolf caught her shoulder with three-inch nails, ripping dark, wet shreds into her jacket. Olivia spun into the attack with a painful-looking maneuver that drug his claws across her arm, but it allowed her to face the cryptid. Her quick grab at his throat slid off as he landed.

I shifted to throw my binding, but the werewolf pivoted with Olivia between us. His head jarred with a punch that flew too fast to register.

My panic had me panting short breaths.

Olivia shot backward, slamming to the ground before me and Mika.

The werewolf's eyes flickered red as I sent the binding spell toward it. With a leap, it avoided my magic and tore at Dagen.

Dagen had shifted so far that her face formed a short muzzle, and a fine fuzz covered her cheeks. She'd been leaping when he attacked, and the force of his strike tossed her into Mika and Phistrel.

I slammed my second shield in front of us just a moment before he jumped for us.

Despite wanting to shriek in fear, I pulled another binding spell and shield.

As the werewolf darted to the side away from me, Phistrel slammed his own shield in place. His breath ragged, he retreated two steps as he reached into Dur-Alf, alighting the mossy realm.

Something more than a rogue werewolf was wrong. My eyes widened, and I gritted my teeth, forcing an unreasonable terror into the pit of my stomach. I'd faced worse with my team. My muscles threatened to lock, but I placed a third shield behind the cryptid, hoping to pin it and set a binding spell.

With a howl, it burst toward Phistrel, but Olivia had recovered and jumped over Dagen to reach the werewolf. She managed two strikes to its massive head before it focused on her.

Scared, I stopped myself from binding them both with my readied spell.

The blast of Mika's weapon, so close to me, startled me. It also drew a layer of the smothering fear away. I spoke in a whisper. "Something's wrong."

Olivia went flying again, struck harder than I imagined a werewolf could manage.

With a flick, I tossed a binding spell, but the werewolf used my own shields to dart behind and avoid it. Muscles both tense and tired, I dug into Dur-Alf.

The entire engagement had lasted less than a minute, but it seemed so much longer. When the werewolf launched away from us, it took a second for me to process. I sped a binding after it, but it had dropped to all fours, zigging and zagging behind the closest trees.

Phistrel's spell missed, as did three shots from Mika. The dark cryptid raced northward, deeper into the woods.

Dagen leaped to follow.

"Don't." Mika's tone carried a weary command.

Dagen growled and stopped, face still shifted to near an animal.

As if a breeze swept it away, the gripping terror left me. "What was that?" I gasped.

"You felt it?" asked Phistrel.

"I've never been that scared," I said. "That's not just a werewolf."

"What?" Dagen's face shifted to human as she turned to us.

Mika had become visible again. "No, I felt something too. Maybe not to the level you describe." They moved toward Olivia, who pushed herself from the ground. "Olivia?"

"No muscle. It'll heal quick. He's stronger than he should be. I don't know about the other." Olivia squinted, studying me. "Panic? Terror? Like a demon's influence?"

"Exactly like that." I sighed. Shame flushed at my cowardliness, but I fought it. A demon could forge emotions inside humans just with their presence.

Phistrel plucked at his beard with a nervous tug. "If I hadn't seen a werewolf, I would have guessed a demon. I nearly ran."

Olivia shook her head. "I've never heard of a demon possessing anyone other than a human, and even that is rare."

The bloody gashes on Olivia's shoulder and upper arm had soaked into dark stains in her blue jacket. Like David, she ignored the pain and moved as if uninjured.

"Perhaps working in conjunction with a werewolf, but what would be the incentive?" My mind couldn't wrap around what we'd just experienced, so I kept scanning the woods around us. Despite being tired from using so much magic, I pulled at Haven and tossed two detection spells, then two more, surrounding us.

"You think a demon might be working with the were-wolf? Perhaps encouraging it?" asked Mika.

When I belatedly realized they addressed me, I twitched. "I guess. I'd rather it not be sitting on top of us." With that comment, I peered up at the sun-speckled canopy, but found only a pair of birds outlined in the white of the detection spell.

Dagen paced around us. "That werewolf was strong, but I'm not sold on the whole demon thing. It could still be newly turned."

Phistrel and I exchanged glances, but didn't argue.

"We'll work both premises for now," said Mika. "I'm going to call in to the locals. They'll be hearing about the gunfire, and I'd rather they weren't out here in the woods."

My chuckle came out unbidden. "Sorry. I grew up in an area like this. No one will call in the shots. Kids, hunters, target practice."

Mika's head cocked back and forth in a shrug, causing the light to glint off glossy black hair. "Okay. I'm still calling in to see if there's anything else we should be alerted about. Meanwhile, figure out what we'll do the next time we're up against this werewolf."

Olivia stepped up to me. "Over a mile south of the previous sighting. He's hunting." She pulled out her cell, scrolling on a map. "There are a couple of residences between here and there. We should check them."

It made sense. "What can we do different? Next time."

My phone rang in my pocket, and I worked it free. "Finn," I explained to Olivia, then answered. "Good morning."

"Not so much. These kids were high, so we've got nothing from them. Pyre and I are going to keep digging. David's getting bored and downright annoying." Finn paused. "Okay to send some of the reports to you? I know you're trying to relax and have the werewolf to deal with."

"Sure." I forced myself not to roll my eyes. "I'll read them when I can." It bothered me that I had missed the case. "We just went up against the werewolf, but lost it." Embarrassment kept me from mentioning the panic.

"Everyone all right?" Finn asked in his southern accent.

"Olivia took a swipe, but says she'll heal." I flashed a smile at her. With a deep inhale, I told him everything. "I panicked. It felt like a demon."

"Doesn't make sense. What does Mika's team think?"

"Mixed. Dagen still thinks it's newly turned."

Finn didn't respond, and muffled voices had the tempo of Marie's quick responses. He cleared his throat. "Pyre's going to check in with Mika about sending out Leah. There's little she can do here, and it sounds like she might be helpful."

I understood Marie's intentions. Leah would offer another werewolf opinion into the mix; an additional option to Dagen's steadfast belief. "Got it."

"Where are you now?" Finn asked.

"In the woods with Mika's team."

"Sorry. I'd hoped you be back with your daughter. What's the plan?"

"I don't know, but Olivia suggested we check out residences between here and the last sighting." I offered her another smile; she didn't return it, and her intense eyes were disarming. "It's the best idea yet."

"All right. We're leaving now. I'm napping while Pyre drives." Finn sounded tired, but I'd have trouble sleeping with her at the wheel.

Mika waved at us to follow, still talking on the phone. We headed back out of the woods with me and Olivia trailing. Dagen grumbled, glaring into the forest and sniffing as she marched.

Phistrel spoke in a hushed tone, and I guessed Mika's call had ended. I pressed harder to catch up.

With a quick glance to make sure we were in earshot, Mika spoke. "We've got two leads. Abandoned car on a mountainside road used by hikers and hunters; waiting for ID on the plates. Second is Ray McMillan, who didn't show up for work yesterday. I'd say split up, but our encounter suggests otherwise."

Olivia responded first. "Missing person."

"Agreed." Mika's phone buzzed, and their eyes

dropped back to me before answering. "Pyre, you checking up on Kristen? We haven't lost her yet."

A moment passed before Mika agreed. "Love to have the extra help. Send Leah out. Could've used her a few minutes ago."

The call ended, and Mika glanced back while pressing through the low branches. "We'll have Pyre's entire team out here soon. The more the merrier is the saying, isn't it?"

"Yep." I couldn't tell if Mika really wanted Leah's help or not. None of their team gave me an odd look, so I assumed it would work out.

Mika continued as the woods thinned enough to see the drive ahead. "Come up with any nifty ways to tackle this werewolf?"

I cleared my throat. "Um, trap it."

Olivia focused a squint at me. "How?"

With a gesture to Phistrel, I continued. "We set binding wards next time we find it, and draw the werewolf to them."

CHAPTER

EIGHT

At our vehicles, we dug out a simple first aid kit, and Olivia used all the gauze to bandage her wounds. Four angry slices had been carved into her shoulder, trailing to three across her bicep. After packing away her bloodied shirt and jacket, she donned a gray sweatshirt.

Once we piled into Mika's Ford, I texted Jade, but she didn't answer. She might be swimming — or ghosting me. With this werewolf on the loose, I could imagine taking her from the trip to assure her safety, or stopping it. I couldn't ignore the danger and go play in the lake.

Olivia sat in the middle, with me on her right next to her wounded shoulder. "He's roving south," she said.

I know. My nod confirmed her deduction. "Closer to the campground. We'll find it."

Mika turned to face us from the front seat. "Let's check out these two leads, then I want to come back here with Dagen, see if we pick up any fresh scents. Kristen, tell me how you see this trap working."

With a pause, I planned my words. "I believe that as

soon as we entered the woods, he hunted us. The werewolf dropped in behind us, probably hiding up in a tree. We can use shields to control it. If we'd set up wards the last time, we could have retreated until it triggered one."

"Hunted us?" asked Mika. "You think he's that confident?"

"Yes." I gestured to Dagen. "He should at least recognize Dagen's scent and know that he faced another werewolf. Right?" That question I posed to Dagen.

"Should. Again, newly turned, he might not understand the smells."

"Still, it attacked five of us."

"We should have chased him." Dagen lowered in her seat, knees against the back of Phistrel's.

Mika shook their head. "We'd taken a beating, and I believe our emotions were adjusted. I didn't react as fast as I might otherwise. It was headed north, away from any houses. Let's see what we have going on with the missing person, then return. I'm up for setting traps next time we go traipsing into the forest."

The trip took longer than I expected as we retraced some of the convoluted path toward the crime scene from the night before, only to turn onto a rugged dirt road part of the way there. My bladder complained, but I kept quiet since Olivia and Dagen had just taken a beating. Still, I was relieved to arrive at the house.

No dogs barked, despite a warning sign out front tacked to a tree trunk. A sun-faded blue Dodge Aspen from the '80s sat on a patch of yellow grass ten yards from the house. The surrounding woods were as thick as those where we'd found the werewolf.

As we stepped out, Mika focused on Dagen. "Anything?" they asked.

Dagen sniffed, walking toward the front door with us

on her heels. "Faint. Days ago. Not even as strong as the house last night."

Mika knocked firmly on the door before Dagen huffed and bolted for the side of the house. Again, we jumped to keep up with her. "What is it, Dagen?"

The sound of flies preceded the smell. A woman's corpse had been dragged to the edge of the woods. Dagen stopped three yards away. "Ray McMillan, I presume." She whipped her phone out and held it high to get a shot of the face. "Body's been out here longer than three days. She died before Paul Bates."

Ray's robe and T-shirt had been ripped down the front to her legs. The body had been gutted, and the gray face attacked postmortem from the lack of blood. A photo might not get much of an ID. "What damage can we attribute to scavengers?" I asked Dagen as she typed.

Olivia peered at the body, getting no closer than any of us. Mika had turned to make a call.

"I'd guess the damage to arms, legs, and face mainly. Mika will get Everek to come over from the other house before we call this in to the locals. This werewolf is hungry. We'll find more bodies." She finished working on her cell and spun toward the house. "Let's check out the building."

I turned, peering at the back door. "It doesn't appear to have been broken into. No dog." With a frown, I pointed at a black water bowl by the steps. "If the werewolf got to the dog, that might be the reason she came out."

We all scanned the unkempt yard up to the surrounding woods. Dagen drew in a deep breath as she headed for the back of the house. Mika gave us a nod while speaking quietly on the cell.

I tugged at Dur-Alf and Mer, checking for wards, and drew a curious glance from Phistrel.

"Still faint," said Dagen as she reached the back door. "Days old." She opened it and paused in the open entry.

The linoleum floor of the kitchen peeled in places, and ancient appliances wore the stains and dents of wear. A reek of rancid milk wafted out, causing me to wrinkle my nose. On the wallpaper of the hallway, a dim reflection of a television flickered, but I heard no sound from it.

When Dagen stepped over the threshold, a yowling black ball flew at her legs.

The burst of motion had me reaching into Dur-Alf with both hands. I must have lurched back, because I bumped into Phistrel.

We shifted in unison as the cat burst through our group like a furry cannonball. Olivia cursed under her breath. The growling feline sped for the woods, never glancing back.

Mika laughed, and I dropped my spells with a blush.

I couldn't tell if Dagen's curse was for Mika or the cat as she marched inside. Olivia followed with her head snapping in sharp motions to take in the kitchen.

Mail, opened and unopened, covered a small dining table, leaving an area for six cat food cans. A cardboard milk container lay on the floor beside the counter, with a thick yellow ring on the floor. Dishes filled the sink. The stench got worse as we entered.

"No scent of werewolf," Dagen offered. "I don't think it ever came inside. Maybe there's no wine." She smiled to herself at the joke.

I moved with purpose into the living room, hoping to escape the smell. The couch had been made up as a bed with the television silently running a documentary beside a potbelly stove. The coffee table had a sleeve of cheap chocolate cookies. It appeared the cat had gnawed on some of them.

The smell hadn't gotten any better. With quick steps, I checked out a bathroom worn from age and two bedrooms stacked with supplies, clothes, and plastic bins. "Nothing in here but junk," I said, heading for the back exit.

Mika stood outside, still talking on the phone, but paused to speak to me. "Another witch. What are the chances?" They didn't wait for a response, returning to their conversation.

"Ray? The dead woman?" The odds were rather unlikely.

Olivia had come out close behind me. "Less than 1 percent of the population can perceive the realms."

I forced a smile, a little put off by her strange way of seeming to follow my thoughts. "What are the odds?"

She frowned. "Greater than one in a hundred."

My nervous laugh just deepened her furrowed eyebrows. "Rhetorical. It is unusual. I don't think a were-wolf can detect a magic user. Must be coincidence." I froze. "A demon though. They might have some sense of it."

"If your perception, and those of Phistrel and Mika, were correct during the last attack, then we should be careful."

A chill crawled up my back as I plucked two quick detection spells from Haven and tossed them into the woods behind the house. Mika cocked their head, curious, but turned to face the trees. Rodents had congregated in the brush, likely feeding off the corpse, but nothing larger lurked there. *No cat, no dog.* The effort drew on my tired energy as I pulled out two more and covered the sides.

Phistrel glowed white with the effect of the spell as he crossed the kitchen toward the back door. He wore a concerned expression as he joined us, studying the woods. "Did I miss something?"

A flush replaced my chill as I explained. "Our newest victim is also a witch. I doubted a werewolf could know that, but a demon might. Just out of caution."

My phone dinged with a text.

Jade had replied with one word.

Swimming.

I sighed. As we'd prepared for the trip, our communication had gotten so much better, until this mess.

Hey honey. Still out with this group. There was another attack. I'm going to be a bit. Sorry.

As I sent the message, I knew she'd be upset. If a demon was involved, and I believed it was, and the werewolf preferred witches, then she might be at risk as much as any of us. Her particular condition came from inadvertently brushing against the Mer realm on a regular basis. Not sure she'd even bother to reply, I sent another text.

Stay safe. I'm worried.

Dagen exited the house while I stared at my cracked screen, and Olivia and Phistrel headed for Mika. The breeze shifted, carrying the haunting, foul reek of Ray's decaying body to me.

"Kid?" Dagen asked.

"Yeah. She's pissed at me."

"How much do you tell her?"

"Nothing about the actual job, but we discuss the dangers out there. She draws the lines back to my work, sometimes."

A heavy engine sounded from the road out front, and Mika started walking with the other two members of the team. Dagen smirked and nudged her head for me to follow. "Everek."

I remembered the name as someone they had coming out to do forensics. "A dwarf?"

"We get him on occasion, when we work in the north. He's a bit eccentric."

"That sounds ominous." As we passed the corner of the house, a red Ram 2500 on a ridiculous lift kit roared down the road, spitting dust. My step faltered at its speed. "Moving fast, isn't he?"

Dagen chuckled.

Mika had reached the victim's car by the time the truck tore into the grass as it stopped beside the team's SUV. The dark tint on the windows hid the dwarf, and the bright rack of lights on the top of the cab didn't help.

We reached the others waiting in front of the house when the door opened and cowboy boots kicked out to find the side bars. A handsome black man jumped down, his head the same height as the bottom of the door. I knew him to be an illusion, but he had an affable smile and charming demeanor. Everek left the truck open as he strode toward us.

His voice started out matching the visage, then morphed into a pitch and tone reminiscent of other dwarves I'd met. "Mika, you've got me running all over this county. I'm dying to see this one, though. Coroner botched the work of your first victim." Everek smiled wider when he caught my eyes. "Kristen Winters. Heard about you. Still raising cows?"

Thanks, Herta, I thought.

CHAPTER

NINE

The others gave me quizzical glances, and I groaned inwardly. "You're friends with Herta?" I asked. Our medical examiner and dwarf, Herta, obviously had associates in the Consociation.

Everek spread his arms in a wide shrug; he stood nearly six feet tall, or his illusion did. "Friends might be a stretch."

"Wonderful. No, no cows." I ignored Dagen's snicker. "Pleasure to meet you, Everek."

He chuckled in a decisively dwarfish tone. "Let's get on with this. Show me the prize."

"Decorum, Everek," Mika chided, adjusting their wire-framed glasses with one finger.

He rolled his eyes. "Please escort me to our corpse."

"Much better."

I let them lead as a team, returning to the backyard. We'd found a single lead from this victim, that there might be a connection to magic usage. *Could that be why the were-wolf attacked us?*

My detection spells had faded to leave only ghostly trails of each of us. Rustling in the brush brought back my concerns, and I dug into Haven to sling two more into the woods. The magic exposed escaping rodents. Phistrel turned to study me with a raised eyebrow, so I gave him a shrug. "Better safe than sorry."

Everek climbed into the brush and straddled Ray's body, his illusion awkwardly placing his knees together. I grimaced at the sight. The air near him hazed brown for a moment, as if he'd drawn from the Earth realm. "A week out. Internal organs were the main feast. Most of the rest is from scavengers. Coyotes, from the smell."

Mika returned to their phone, checking a message. "We've got an ID on the abandoned vehicle. Willy Snyder."

"A witch?" I asked.

With a pleased appraisal, Mika nodded to me. "Yes. Thoughts?"

"That the demon is targeting witches," I said.

"Odd, but workable with what we have. Uses the werewolf. But why?"

"I don't know." I wished our operations tech, Tomas, was on comms with me, even if he treated me like crap most of the time. He would explain, with appropriate disdain and abundant snark, the obvious. "We're building a timeline, though. The hiker, Willy, is first on our present list, then Ray and Paul. We need to get with a local coven; they might map out the witches in the area for us."

Mika agreed, speaking to Phistrel. "Any contacts?"

"In Montana?" Phistrel huffed. "I've got a friend in San Francisco. That's as far north as I go."

"Check in with Neddie, then." Mika turned. "I'm calling this in, Everek."

"I'll ask some people," I offered. Yaz, our coven priestess in Grand Junction, had the widest network of witches of anyone I'd ever met. If she didn't have any names, my old coven in Oregon might help.

"Go for it." Mika tilted their head as if with a thought. "While you are at it, can you message Tomas to see if a demon would have any reason to target witches? He's got a head for facts."

I groaned inside, but smiled. "Sure. Happy to."

Olivia hovered near Everek, watching his illusion work. Dagen paced the yard. I dialed Yaz, wondering about the time difference.

She answered on the first ring with her usual affable tone. "Morning, love. Surprised to see you calling."

"I'm on a case out in Montana. Are you busy, or can you talk?"

"Enjoying tea out back in the garden. What can I help with?"

"We've had two witches killed, looking into a third, here in Flathead County in Montana, and I'd like to speak with a local coven."

"Is it. .. ?" Yaz trailed off, knowing I wouldn't be able to give her a ton of details. Since my job at the DRC, I'd called her a few times with questions, but wouldn't go into specifics. "Okay. I've got someone who used to live in Kalispell about seven years back. Guessing they still do. Going to text you their number after."

I ached to ask her about demons hunting witches, but the Consociation would not want that public. "Thanks, Yaz."

"No problem. How's the kid?"

My lips tightened, not wanting to admit it, but I'd been close with Yaz. "We're on a camping trip with a friend of hers, and I'm sort of screwing it up by helping with an investigation. We've got to stop it, though."

"Damn, sorry to hear. That must be messing you up.

You're a good mom, Kristen. You've done her right — balancing a career. It's tough."

"Well, she's not happy."

"Teens aren't. Ever."

"I'll check in with you later. After this is over." I peered around as Everek moved from the body to speak with Mika and the team. Dagen had stopped pacing to listen.

Yaz and I said quick goodbyes, and I ambled over.

"No doubt about it being a werewolf?" asked Mika.

"None. Even a mundane human will have difficulty classifying this as a bear." Everek flashed me a toothy smile as I approached.

Dagen scoffed. "Already did with Paul Bates."

Olivia kept back from Everek. *Dwarves and vampires*, I thought. My phone dinged with a text, likely Yaz, but I ignored it for the moment.

"Anyway, the attack is unusual as the first bites were all focused on the abdomen, as if the werewolf was too hungry to bother killing its prey first."

"Newly turned," Dagen said with satisfaction.

Mika flicked a glance at me, and I asked, "Why wouldn't she just bind it?"

Everek's illusion shrugged in a sloppy imitation of a six-foot human. "A viable question that I can't answer, but you knew that." He pointed toward the house. "Need me to get my kit and go in there?"

"He never went inside." Dagen scanned the woods. "It's gone south. We should be hunting it."

The dwarf scratched at its chin, making the illusion perform the odd maneuver of digging at a shaved face. "Well, I'm almost done with a preliminary report for the first victim. I will spoil it with the fact that I believe the werewolf enjoyed two meals. During the initial kill, and then post imbibing."

From Dagen's frown, I knew this additional information didn't mix well with her assumptions.

Mika's eyes flicked to each of us. "Thank you, Everek. Can you stay in the area afterward? I'm hoping we won't need you, but you know how these cases get."

"Of course. There's a museum I'd like to visit." He took her question as a dismissal and strode for his monster truck.

Phistrel held up his cell. "Neddie's got three local witches who have been here for a decade and show recent social activity."

I didn't mention my text from Yaz.

"I'm calling in the body," said Mika. "When the locals get here, we're off."

While Dagen began pacing the backyard again, I dialed my home office for Tomas. My body tensed, and I forced a smile, as if he would see it.

He let my call ring for a minute. "Yes?"

"Hi, Tomas. We're, uh, working a case out here in Montana."

"I know." He interrupted between my breaths.

"And, I wondered, if there's ever been evidence that a demon will target witches."

"Yes." From his tone, he might as well of said, "Of course."

My eyebrows raised. "Why?"

"Wouldn't know. They don't interview well."

I ignored his bland quip. "How about in cases where the victim has been eaten?"

Tomas paused. "There have been cross-references between those demons who appear to enjoy eating human flesh. I can think of three cases in the past six hundred years."

"Could you send me the details, and I'll look them up on—" My phone dinged with a text.

"Yes. I'm busy."

"I appreciate that. How is the team's case going?" I pulled my phone away, peering at the screen. Tomas had already hung up.

With an exaggerated exhale, I swiped over to my texts. With the one from Yaz, I noted the name and replied, Thanks. Tomas had been considerate enough to provide links for his reference, but I had to log into the database first. It lagged, and I scanned the surrounding woods. We'd kept coverage through much of the investigation, but that didn't mean we had any bandwidth.

I hadn't noticed Phistrel head to the car, but he returned with an armful of water bottles, and I gladly accepted one. We'd burned through half the morning, and my body wanted me to sit after expending energy on magic.

The first case that Tomas sent dealt with a demon who had eaten five members of a coven in Nebraska in 1798. Three of the those remaining killed it with binding and fire, but the Consociation author gave no opinion on the reasoning of the demon. Her report appeared clinical, so I delved into the rabbit hole of her other entries through a slagging program. A Merfolk, she'd written no books in which I hoped her theories might emerge.

"There we go," Mika announced as a white SUV pulled beside our Ford. A second and third vehicle crowded our chances of pulling out neatly. "Phistrel, move the car before they bring in the entire sheriff's department."

Without a word, he jogged toward the officers piling out. Rebekah was among them, waving at us like we'd met at a picnic.

Olivia sidled up to me. "Did Tomas have anything?"

"Yes, but I'm digging through for why, more than for the details of the actions."

"Was a werewolf involved?"

"Not on the first case. The demon possessed a human who owned an inn. She used knives to carve out the flesh. It was all one coven as well."

"Was the innkeeper familiar or in conflict with the coven?"

"That wasn't mentioned. The case was in 1798. Certain aspects were very detailed, but not everything I might like."

"Unfortunate," said Olivia.

Mika waited as Rebekah led a surly older man toward us. His weathered skin hung from his scowl. Two younger deputies followed, the woman carrying a forensic kit.

Rebekah kept her affable smile as she introduced the man. "Sheriff Buckley's got the other case. He'll lead on this."

The unhappy man had a worn demeanor, but sharp eyes that noted each of us. "How'd you find the body?" he asked.

"Oh, they was asking about any missing persons," Rebekah offered.

Buckley huffed and walked past us toward the body. I couldn't see his expression as he stopped a yard from Ray's corpse, but his bent frame straightened. "FWP needs to get moving. When this gets out, people will be clamoring to hunt every bear in the county. Those drunk idiots will be everywhere."

He appeared to be speaking to himself, but Rebekah answered. "Like that wolf three years ago."

The surly face intact, Buckley spun, focused on Mika. "What's the FBI's piece in all this?"

Mika managed a stiff, professional smile. "As we explained in our original correspondence, we're not assured by the findings of your medical examiner's report. We can't afford to have any murders go without investigation."

His eyes squinted into a glare. "Bullshit. Feds. Always up to something."

"Nonetheless," Mika answered.

As the other two deputies arrived, the younger man had appeared nervous, especially around Buckley, while the woman quietly masked and gloved out of her kit.

"FWP?" I asked Buckley, in part to break his focus on Mika.

"Fish, Wildlife, and Parks," said Rebekah.

"They'll bring in hunters?" The idea of sending drunk men into the woods for the werewolf to feast on seemed like an unwise plan.

"Wrangle them, more's like." She chuckled. "We're about a quarter of a mile from Paul Bate's place, so the area will be thick in a couple days with yahoos."

Buckley moved back to the corpse, grumbling under his breath.

Mika's smile grew more natural. "Well, we want to check on that abandoned vehicle."

"Oh, yeah. Let me make sure it ain't been towed. Wait, what you turn up out by Red Owl Trail? Something got those dogs all squirrelly, and Anna says she saw bigfoot again."

"Nothing," Mika assured the sheriff. It made sense, with hunters interested, not to send them where we'd encountered the werewolf.

Rebekah accepted the answer and called in to find out that they hadn't towed the vehicle yet, with some commentary about the "boys" being busy, but they'd get around to it.

It took ten more minutes to cleave ourselves from the scene and pile into the Ford. Phistrel had moved it in time as three more vehicles arrived from the sheriff's office and a nosy, local man in a pickup.

"We should head back to where we know the werewolf is," argued Dagen.

I didn't disagree. What would we learn about the driver of the truck without spending the day in the woods? The werewolf had ranged farther south, closer to the campground. I'd never be able to convince the Turners to get the kids out of there unless the FWP recommended it. Did the Consociation have sway there?

"It's a twenty-minute round trip, maybe thirty. I just want you to give me a sniff. See if we've got cause to believe this is related. Then we head back and maybe send Kristen and Phistrel off to meet with local witches. Grab us some lunch while they're out." Mika clicked their seatbelt, then twisted to peer back at me. "You okay hanging with us a while longer? I know this is messing with your time with your daughter."

She's already pissed. I'd rather she be safe and angry, I thought, but kept my response simple. "Of course."

TEN

As the SUV pulled away from the mass of cars, I jerked my head toward the window where blue flashed in the woods deep behind the victim's property. If the angle had been right, I could have seen a reflection of one of the sheriff's vehicles, but that didn't seem the case.

I craned to study the shadows between the trees, drawing Mika's attention. "What is it?"

With a wave of my hand, I dismissed it. "I thought I saw a flash in the woods."

"Scene photos."

The placement wasn't correct, but it wouldn't likely be connected to a ravenous werewolf that we'd just had a skirmish with miles away. "Probably."

Satisfied, Mika focused on Dagen. "Let's talk about this newly turned werewolf theory."

"Hypothesis," Olivia corrected.

"Don't start." Mika chuckled, then lowered their voice to a serious tone. "Does all the evidence still fit? Be critical of your own idea."

Despite the bumpy road, Olivia twisted next to me, pulling water from a cooler in the back. Whenever she moved beside me, she took care not to bump into me and expose Tarus. I appreciated her consideration.

As she accepted one of the waters and opened it, Dagen finally spoke. "There are questionable moments, like stopping for wine between feedings, but that would also be difficult for a drug-addled werewolf as well."

Mika remained focused on Dagen without inviting us into the conversation. "How does the demonic influence impact your premise?"

Over the water bottle, Dagen flicked a glance at me, then finished her sip and stared into the open container. "I don't know that we have enough evidence to be sure that we are dealing with a demon. It seems likely, considering our one encounter. If Kristen hadn't mentioned something, I'd just assume Phistrel was being a chicken-shit."

He huffed from the driver's seat.

The quiet that followed pronounced the rough road we drove down that jostled my bladder. With care, I sipped my water while Olivia watched Mika. Dagen's question of whether we had encountered a demon forced me to examine my own assumptions. The panic had been abnormal; after being on the force and part of the DRC team, I knew my emotional reactions. My first instinct had been a demon because their interactions and ability to sway human emotions were well documented. They could incite from panic to rage. What else could instill unusual panic? Mika had felt something.

"The other witches did not bind the werewolf when attacked, which could support our panicked experience. If not a demon, what else would cause atypical fear?" I wouldn't be calling Tomas about this question.

Phistrel cleared his throat. "Semet's Heart."

Mika tilted their head, agreeing.

"I was pretty up close and personal with the dude, and he wasn't wearing jewelry."

Dagen chuckled.

"It could have been under that fur," Olivia said.

We turned onto a paved road, but I still had to pee, so I mentioned it.

Phistrel nodded, answering without checking Mika. "I'll stop at the market, where we picked you up last night."

I considered a cup of coffee, as it had to be better in the middle of the day. When we arrived in a few minutes, the entire team trailed in, but they let me hit the bathroom first. We hadn't resolved the determination of whether or not a demon was involved, nor whether the werewolf had been newly turned. None of our ideas rang true to me, like puzzle pieces that we kept trying to force together.

Dagen took the bathroom next. "Mika's buying. Hot dogs look good."

I preferred pizza, but I doubted we'd be waiting for them to cook one. While I mixed cream and sugar into a coffee, Jade texted.

Heading back for lunch.

I grimaced. She'll want me to join them, at least for part of the day. I was ruining this for her.

I can't make it back yet. There's been another attack.

We heard they closed the hiking trails. Can't they handle this without you?

I'd rather make sure it's caught. Otherwise, I wouldn't want you here. Have the Turners considered leaving?

My hand automatically swirled the coffee, waiting for a response, until I realized there might not be one. I capped the coffee, keeping my phone out as I searched for the others.

With a casual wave at my coffee to the attendant, Mika waited at the front with an arrangement of snacks and beverages.

My cell pinged with a belated response from Jade.

I'M NOT LEAVING.

With two more texts, I tried to explain the danger, without explaining anything. Frustrated, I piled into the SUV with a quick lunch and passable coffee.

It only took a few minutes for Phistrel to drive the Ford up to the turnoff with three vehicles, one belonging to Willy Snyder.

The mountains loomed to the east, and the air held the scent of pine, reminding me of my childhood. If it got any warmer, I'd be taking off my jacket. The wet ground spoke of a morning rain.

Dagen circled the car. "I've got nothing here," she said. "Can we go back now?"

Mika's head bobbed from one shoulder to the next. "So he's out there in the woods."

I pointed through the window. "I'd guess there's two of them." There were two coffee cups in the holder, and a large takeout bag crumpled on the floor of the passenger's side.

Phistrel stepped up and checked the locked car door. He raised his eyebrows at Mika, who nodded. He pulled an unlocking spell from the blue Mer realm and splashed it along the passenger side.

Dagen grunted and stuck her head inside as he opened the door. "Male and female. Week old. Someone likes cinnamon buns." She popped out and leaned on the car. "We know where it is. Finding these bodies will not stop it.

We should go back to where we fought it and set up some traps, like Kristen suggested."

With one last look at the surrounding forest, Mika relented, motioning us back to the vehicle.

A cold, professional side of me agreed with Dagen, while another wanted closure for Willy and his hiking partner. They would be found, once we finished; even before then, but it didn't make leaving feel any less callous. For all we knew, they were only injured, though I doubted any of us believed it.

"Where? Can you text me the address?" Mika got the call while we drove down the slope, putting Deputy Rebekah on speaker.

"Will do. Buckley's in a bit of a mood, if you know what I mean."

"I can imagine. How many?"

"Just Gary. His wife was up in Kalispell with her sister. She got lucky, though she might not see it."

"Last name?" Mika asked.

"Oh, Atkins, like the diet."

"Thank you, Rebekah. Do you have a time of death yet?"

"Had to be after 8:30 this morning. That's when she left."

I checked my watch. At 11:23 a.m., the attack had to have happened after our encounter. If we had stopped the werewolf, then Gary Atkins would be alive. Dagen wasn't wrong. We'd wasted time heading to check on the abandoned car.

ELEVEN

I sat beside Olivia, running the timeline in my head. "It's feeding every other day."

Phistrel didn't drive with the same reckless behavior as Marie, but she was a dragon-shifter. We returned down the same street we'd arrived on, surrounded by trees and glimpses of mountains, with only the occasional business or homes dotting the sides of the road.

Mika swiveled, facing us, eyes darting behind the wire-rimmed glasses. "Does that fit your concept, Dagen? I've found few details about newly turned werewolves gone rogue, but I'm assuming it's a regular warning in your circles."

Dagen sat up, rather than sliding into one of her more languid positions. "Every day would be more likely."

"Perhaps supplementing on wild game?" I suggested.

Olivia turned to me. "We don't know that we have found all the kill sites. Paul's door alerted a local mail carrier, we followed a no-show to Ray, and the car's been abandoned for a week."

I frowned, worried that she might be right. In rural areas, a lone person, or even a couple, might not be missed for days.

"What are you thinking?" asked Mika.

"Is Gary Atkins a witch?"

Mika lifted their cell. "Waiting to find out."

"If he is," I emphasized the phrase, "then we've got enough pattern to predict targets. The werewolf is moving south, but not traveling as fast as it could. While picking its quarry."

"That quarry being witches," said Olivia.

"Exactly. So we find these locals and map out the witches as best we can. Your Neddie could start plotting us a map between those that the Consociation has locations for within the range and path of the werewolf. We set traps there."

"Me likes," said Mika. "I see why Marie wants you on her team. I'll trade Dagen here for you."

"Bite me," Dagen said with a chuckle.

"Said the werewolf to the Mer." Mika turned to the front, typing on their phone.

My cell dinged with a report forwarded by Mika. The Consociation had identified Gary Atkins as a witch and his wife as an arcane practitioner. Another message followed with a map that marked the location of the deaths with dates that showed the werewolf moved southerly by the day. It took a moment to discern that orange dots indicated possible residences of witches. Some were brighter, with a high percentile next to them, and others duller, with low numbers. *Probabilities that they were still there.* With Phistrel's and Yaz's lists, we might be able to solidify the scores.

"This will help." I tilted my head to speak over the headrest to Mika. "We've got a day, maybe two, before the werewolf will strike again." Jade's camping trip would be nearly over by then, and I didn't see myself spending much time at the site.

Olivia had pulled out her own phone while I'd been zooming in and out on the map. It appeared they had their own reporting system and database. "Are we going to be interviewing the local covens this afternoon?"

"Unless we get a better plan," answered Mika.

"Hunt the damned thing." Dagen's frustration seethed in her tone.

We were traveling down familiar roads back toward Swan Lake. I'd grown accustomed to traffic, especially since working with the DRC in Atlanta, but here the occasional truck or car reminded me of my time in Oregon. As a witch, I'd known of werewolves and vampires, even Merfolk, but the threatening cryptids had been no more than anecdotes of warning. The Consociation had been more theory than a shadow government. However, here I was, hunting a man-eating werewolf and possibly a demon. I'd been painfully naïve.

"Leah's going to arrive in a few hours. We'll need to pick her up." Mika sounded pleased. "I'm still not sure if I'll split us up after she gets here. Having one more team member who can't be affected will be a bonus."

Dagen, still perched in her seat, took a breath as if to comment, but stopped. Her opinions of our reactions weren't clear, but she didn't buy into the premise of a demon. Because of that, I wanted to remain critical of my assumptions.

Olivia, still focused on the map, spoke. "I'm not confident we'll be able to rely on setting a trap at a specific location. The attacks weren't at *all* the locations where witches resided along the range of the werewolf's movement. Two would have been likely candidates that we should check in on. The hypothesis assumes the frequency of feeding, which could be inaccurate."

Mika twisted about to pay attention. "Noted. Identify them for Neddie and request she try to confirm their status. We'll circle back to them if we don't have a positive response. I'm uncomfortable backtracking when we've got any chance of stopping this werewolf. Too many balls in the air."

Phistrel slowed, waiting for a pickup to pass from the other direction before making a turn down another dirt road. A gate had been left open. The mountains climbed into the horizon ahead of us, then spiking pines blocked them as we turned south.

Olivia spoke as she typed. "I'm your best bet to split off from the group."

"Not on the menu," snarked Dagen.

As she sent a message, Olivia frowned, as if confused. "The werewolf's?"

"No offense, but you don't smell appetizing. Even a newly turned werewolf would have second thoughts."

"What I was referring to was my ability to heal from egregious wounds, but your point is sound."

With a flat-lipped expression, Mika failed to hide a smile. "I agree, Olivia. Let's see what our plan is after we visit the scene. How much longer, Phistrel?"

"Google says thirteen minutes." From his right hand holding the wheel, he pointed an index finger down the road. "Rained here last night or early this morning, so we might have conditions that slow us down." As he spoke, we thudded through a rut, jarring my back.

Closer to twenty minutes later, we pulled up to the same cluster of sheriff's vehicles we'd left at Ray's house. The winding road up the slope had flattened over the last few miles, letting us park on a deceptively level stretch of grass at the foot of the mountains.

Gary Atkins's house appeared to have been built a hundred years prior and patched every decade or so. The shiny black paint of the newer Chevy truck parked out front set a sharp contrast against the faded beige of the building. The sheriff and deputies clustered at one vehicle where Buckley sat in the driver's seat. He frowned as we pulled up.

Before we'd come to a full stop, Rebekah split off from the group and strode toward us with her trademark smile. It seemed she'd been designated as our liaison.

Dagen popped out on her side once Phistrel shifted into park, her nostrils flaring. Only exhaust and pine wafted in the air when I stepped out with Mika.

"Oh, yeah," called Dagen. "Fresh."

I scanned the encroaching woods. *How rash would this werewolf be?* Could it hold a grudge against us? If Dagen were correct, it might be satiated and wandering in the hills. As I turned south, my thoughts drifted to Jade eating lunch with the Turners, not knowing what truly lurked in the woods.

Fifty yards away, blue flashed in the shadows of the forest to the left of the Atkinses' house. "Did you see that?" I barked in a loud voice.

Rebekah, in her cheerful tone, and Olivia, with a sharp inquisitive note, both asked, "See what?"

I flushed, flicking my focus to them, then back to the woods, before missing anything. "Maybe a deer."

"Folks been seeing bigfoot about here lately. Got seven reports just over the past two days, but we get them every once in a while." Rebekah laughed as she spoke.

Mika cleared their throat. "So, is Mrs. Atkins here? I'd like to interview her before we check the crime scene."

"Heavens, no. We sent her off once we pulled up. She's in quite a state."

I couldn't take my eyes off the woods. A chill crawled up my neck, as if something stared back at me. Perhaps I could get closer under some premise and toss a Haven detection spell there. *Last thing I need is to bring the werewolf out.* The Consociation preferred we didn't involve dangerous cryptids and the mundane. A sheriff and five deputies as witnesses would be frowned upon, if they survived.

Dagen had come up on my other side, leaving three of Mika's team staring, while Mika tried to distract Rebekah.

"All right. We'll get her information later. So, what do we have inside?" Mika clasped Rebekah on the shoulder, turning her toward the building.

"It's gruesome." Rebekah took a hesitant step, glancing back. "Tore Gary apart."

Phistrel marched with her and Mika. "Tore apart?" he asked.

Olivia whispered, "What?"

"A blue flash. I saw it earlier when we left Willy's abandoned car."

"Crap," swore Dagen. "I thought you had something." The muscles in her jaw rippled before she spun to follow the others.

"Blue? As in Mer?" asked Olivia, still keeping her voice low.

Was it? "Maybe. I'm not imagining it." I didn't feel panicked. That was a good sign.

"Doubt you would. You've got a sharp eye."

We stood a moment longer, then Olivia continued. "Tore apart?"

With a sigh, I began moving toward the house. "Do you suppose we pissed it off?"

Buckley, waiting until Mika and Phistrel passed the cluster of deputies, called, "I'm calling in to your people. I still don't know what reason you're out here chasing a bear. It ain't right."

Mika just smiled and nodded, never breaking stride.

He scowled harder. "Don't mess with the crime scene."

Olivia and I jogged to Dagen, as if to catch up, but in truth, I didn't want to deal with an angry man's ego. Buckley grumbled something to the other officers in a sour tone.

The front of the house had been planted with well-tended, fragrant flowers and herbs that hinted at both a witch and an arcane practitioner. With tugs at Dur-Alf and Mer, I checked for wards, surprised to find Dur-Alf glyphs on the windows. As simple alarms, they would have let Gary know if someone tried to break in. Nothing on the door, but he'd have to reset it constantly.

"Any sign of entry?" Mika asked Rebekah.

"Nope. Day like today, Gary might have left the door open for the air."

The temperature seemed to be in the fifties, and with the cloud cover, might not rise much more. To people in Atlanta, that would be chilly, but we were in the mountains.

From my view outside the door, the bloodbath inside had sprayed the walls and left a residue of ruddy red. The same young man from Ray's murder scene knelt at a coffee table with an evidence bag. He wasn't wearing booties. The local enforcement still thought of this as an animal attack. Marie would have likely pried the entire investigation from Buckley's fingers and had local FBI dragged into the mix.

I paused at the entrance as the rest of the team

entered. My nonchalant gaze into the nearby woods failed as I found Olivia studying me, not the scene.

In his living room, Gary Atkins lay in three distinct pieces. I winced, imagining the wife walking into this sight. His body rested against wet cushions of the couch with his midsection hollowed out in shreds, missing much of his internal organs. The left arm had been severed at the elbow and tucked into the corner as if digging for change.

His head had been ripped off, smashed into a television that blocked the north window, and left to drop to the floor. Splintered lines on the screen hinted at the force, as well as the misshapen dent in the victim's temple.

Mika addressed the woman preparing a large evidence bag. "The head looks like it was ripped free."

"I'd not want to make a determination on that. The coroner will."

"Understood. Leave it then. I have my examiner driving in now."

The woman, a tech despite her deputy's uniform, exchange glances with her coworker. "I'll need to check in with Sheriff Buckley."

"By all means." With a step to the side, Mika made space, prompting the rest of us to move out of the way and into the dining room where only a few drops of blood had spattered.

Buckley did not seem like the kind of man to let the "Feds" interfere more than we already were. I'd met his kind working for the DRC and on the force in Grand Junction. As the tech moved for the door, I stepped down the hall. At the rear of a cluttered mud room, the back door stood open.

Against the trees lining the backyard, the engine of Everek's monster truck echoed.

TWELVE

I studied the floor with Olivia shadowing me. "No tracks. I guess it went back out the front door."

She still stepped with care, eyes darting from the hung jackets to my eyes. "I'm more curious about what you saw in the woods."

Me too. I stepped outside to hear Buckley swear from the front while Everek's engine roared and whined with a hint of tires against dirt. "Let's take a peek." I tugged two Haven spells from the realm, ignoring the dull headache that rose with the exertion.

As I tossed them both into the woods where I'd seen the blue spark, another blue light flashed, close to the edge of the trunks I could see.

"There." Olivia dashed past me at the abnormal speed of a vampire.

My spells hit, lighting a few small rodents, but nothing bigger than rabbits. Olivia's form glowed as it whisked into range. The color had not been that of Mer, a blue that leaned into green. The shade reminded me of the cobalt Larkspur that grew in Oregon.

As Buckley yelled through his tantrum on the other side of the house, Dagen burst past me, chasing Olivia. Everek's truck revved out front, then turned off.

Phistrel stepped beside me, watching Dagen catch up to Olivia, who stood at the forest's edge. "See something?" he asked.

"Blue flash."

"Never believed in bigfoot."

"What?"

"I had a roommate, a mundane on the edge of arcane, who loved them. A blue flash is part of the lore. It varies."

"Now that you mention it, I remember a vague description, but had never given it any thought." I watched Dagen sniffing and grew curious. With a glance back inside, I strode toward the woods, leaving Phistrel standing there.

The ruckus at the front had quieted as I crunched through shin-high grass. Olivia watched Dagen, as did I. As I approached, our werewolf team member crouched in the woods, close to where I'd seen the flash.

Dagen spoke when I was a few yards away. "A second werewolf. I knew I'd smelled two earlier." She glowed with Haven as she tracked a scent back toward the road, reaching the point where I'd seen the first blue light. "Fresh." With a frown, she marched back in wide loops, nostrils flaring.

"Outside of the one path, she lost the scent." Olivia scanned about us with sharp jerks of her head, but kept Dagen in her focus.

With each snort from Dagen, I agreed. She'd pass into the initial path, walk a pace or two, and return. I remained silent as she returned to the place where the second flash had come from, three yards into the trees between twin pines. Why the flash? Where had it gone so quickly? A demon, unbound, could fade to the edge of a realm, unseen beyond a slight disturbance in matter, but that did not explain what she smelled, nor the blue flash.

"Damn it." Dagen dropped to her knees and palms to smell the ground. "Its strong. I'd have to guess female. But only from one spot to the other. I can't track it arriving or leaving."

My headache hung dull over my eyes, hampering my thoughts. The regular use of the realms and my encounter with unnatural panic had taken a toll. "It doesn't make sense," I said.

Olivia eyed me, lowering her eyebrows. "Witches need rest between touching the realms. However, I am baffled by the data points as well."

Dagen's cell rang, and she pulled it out with a scowl. "Yes?" As she listened, she pointed to the house. "Okay. We'll be there."

I turned, assuming Mika had called, and joined Olivia on our return. Dagen headed for the front rather than the back door, so we adjusted, keeping up with her angry march.

As always, the pieces needed to fit together, but I'd grown used to Tomas and Marie having a wealth of experience that I could draw upon. "Have any of you ever heard of a blue flash before? Maybe in connection to a demon?"

"It was another werewolf," Dagen said with a growl.

Without an argument, I checked Olivia, who shook her head. Everek fired up his truck, revving it. A plume of smoke drifted over the house and the sheriff's vehicles parked out front. Kicking dust, the red monster truck barreled down the road ahead of us, disappearing behind the edge of the trees in moments.

Mika and Phistrel turned the corner of the house and

paused when we were in sight. "Nothing that wasn't expected from Everek," Mika said. "The head and arm were ripped from the body."

Dagen huffed. "I told you it was strong."

"Never argued the point. I want to track it. First, tell me about the blue light Phistrel saw."

"Got a second damned werewolf," Dagen said.

Mika's eyes flicked between the three of us. "Did you see it?"

"Smelled it. I'll lay a hundred bucks that it's a she."

Still grouped by the vehicles, the deputies watched us. Buckley sat in his front seat again, holding court with a perpetual glaring scowl in our direction. I gave Mika a breakdown of what I'd witnessed from the moment I'd thrown the Haven spells, then returned to the flash I'd seen on arrival. Dagen confirmed my positioning as the points and trail she could scent of the new werewolf.

"I told you I smelled two, right off the bat," Dagen added.

"Disturbing," said Mika. "Phistrel, hit up Neddie and see if there's anything in the archive that matches, outside the mundane human lore that you mentioned."

"We tracking it?" asked Dagen. "The first one, that is. I'm done with this bullshit. Chasing our tails like a Bull Terrier."

"We are. I'd like to get lucky. Everek says the scene is fresh. We might have a period of time before it strikes again."

"Maybe it's full and taking a nap." The comment brought a hint of a smile to Dagen's lips.

Mika led us back to the front door, ignoring the deputies, and Dagen's nostrils twitched. We followed as a group out to the drive, then east into the woods. The mountains loomed ahead of us, but the slope didn't incline until after we crossed the road where it passed the property.

"Let us know where you think will be good to set Kristen's trap." Mika's statement could have been for any of us.

I glanced at Phistrel, hoping he had some reserves left.

Our path turned south, forcing us into a stilted pace with one foot stepping higher up the slope. The moist pine needles and ground gave way underfoot, causing me to slow. A few yards deeper into the mountain, the pitch angled sharp enough that I'd not be comfortable climbing it. At a small clearing, I could see the end of a ridge that rose above us.

I skidded to a stop when Dagen pulled up short, dropping to sniff at the ground.

"Dagen?" Mika asked.

"I've got two of them suddenly. Male and female. It just popped up."

My fingers glided into Dur-Alf, and I pulled out a shield and a binding, fighting the weariness. "Moving together?" I asked.

"No, her scent is fresher. I'd guess twenty minutes, but he came through here maybe half an hour ago. We're not close."

Was she hunting him, like us? Partners? "Does that make sense to you?"

Dagen frowned at my question. "Perhaps. If she were part of the Biera that helped him turn, she might be trying to find him as well."

Her premise assumed a newly turned werewolf, which we didn't have a confirmation of, only Dagen's belief. I kept my point to myself.

"We should have Neddie locate any local werewolves as well. It might lead to your Biera." Mika drew out their cell, then pocketed it. "No reception. I should have loaded a map."

Olivia gestured to our right. "We're parallel to the road. You can see it every once in a while."

Phistrel pulled out his phone. "Nothing much up here in the direction we're headed. Sixmile Mountain is to our left. Southeast of us doesn't have any residences until you get to the shore of Swan Lake."

Or south to the campground.

We'd hiked twenty minutes before Dagen's trail dropped steeply down, exposing a section of gray rock on the mountainside. Mika stopped us, holding a tree trunk to peer down to the south, then west. "That's a good climb. They went this way, Dagen?"

"We're less than half an hour behind him now. We can make it down. She did. We're getting closer to both of them. Her scent is so fresh."

From our vantage, we could see down twenty yards to the flat ground at the base and through the thin stretch of trees to where the land folded into more sharp drops and rises. Stone frequently pierced the forest floor, jutting up in dabs of gray against the summer green. The mountain range blocked the east with a forbidding wall.

I held the trunk of a pine with my right hand and rested against it. Somewhere three or four miles ahead, Jade ate lunch with the Turners. *Too close.* Maybe with this many known deaths from a "man-eating bear," the campground would shut down until the "bear" was caught.

"I'm calling it," said Mika. "We head back. Get some information from the local covens. Plot some data. Pick up Leah. Look for a local werewolf and Biera. Half an hour's lead is too much in this terrain."

"We wait for it to kill again?" asked Dagen.

I didn't like the idea, but we might hike for the next

half of the day without catching up. "How long can it keep going?" I asked Dagen.

"If it is fully transmogrified? In animal form? For the rest of the day." Her tone carried her frustration. She knew as well as we did that even if we climbed down, we'd have little chance of catching up unless he stopped.

Olivia spoke as she leaned over the drop, searching below. "With another werewolf on his trail, he might not rest until dark."

Dagen paced a restless circle, sniffing. "She's so close."

I frowned, focusing below as Olivia was. The sun easily pierced the thin canopy on the slope, but the ground angled sharply in spots, hiding the forest floor. Someone could hide below us without effort. My hands whipped into Haven, and the drain of energy combined with my thoughtless release of the trunk.

I swayed, misstepped, and the moist ground slid out from underneath me. My squawk caused Olivia to straighten, but even her quick snatch missed me as I slipped ass first down the slope. Pitched like I was on a water slide, it was a mistake to grab at a tree as I passed. First, I already moved too fast; second, it spun me to my side.

Needles and mud shoved up my pant leg, but I managed a pivot and dragged my heels against the forest floor. Experienced at tumbling while hiking, I used hands and feet like rudders to keep from rolling sideways.

Close to the bottom, the ground disappeared. I scraped over one of the ridges I'd seen from above; spinning and flailing, I slammed onto the flat base. I lifted my head, spit out needles, and drew a sharp, deep breath.

Three feet from my face, a cryptid crouched in a rocky alcove. Its hair was shaggy, and its face more ape-like than lupine. Light gray eyes were wide in what appeared surprise at my sudden appearance.

Bigfoot?

She, I assumed, raised her fingers and dug into gray Ya Keya. A brilliant blue flash sparked from the contact.

With a snap, the cryptid disappeared.

THIRTEEN

I lay muddied, staring at the empty space in the rocks. Roots from a nearby tree dangled from the earthen overhang, and the stone shone wet at the bottom. Aches and scrapes introduced themselves to my mind. "Oww."

"Kristen?" Mika called.

My dulled wits identified someone climbing down the slope I'd used as a water slide. "It just disappeared," I said. My heart skipped in panic, and I shoved to my side with a bruised hand. I pulled a detection spell from Haven and dropped it on myself. A glow surrounded me and marked Dagen climbing down at a good clip, but no one else. "Not an illusion." I'd never heard of someone being able to travel with a snap, but I'd been able to shift realms.

"Are you okay?" Mika yelled.

"Yeah, yes." I winced as I climbed to my knees. "No, not really."

"Wait there. We're coming."

I rolled onto my butt. "Sounds good." Most of my aches were on my back and side. If I'd had the energy, I would have stood, but that could wait. "She was down here. Not a werewolf, I don't think."

"What?" Dagen yelled the closest, but the chorus included Olivia and Mika.

I rolled my head back. "It wasn't a werewolf, but hairy. I think it's what Dagen's been smelling." With more effort, I spoke louder. "It snapped its fingers with a blue spark and disappeared." Eyes closed, my eyebrows raised. "Could it have been eavesdropping on us?"

Dagen dropped beside me. "How do you know it wasn't a werewolf?"

"When you partially morph, the bridge of your nose extends, as if creating a muzzle. Sorry, if that's rude. Hers, its face, was dead flat, like a gorilla's. Hair was way longer."

With a touch to her nose, Dagen considered my statement before speaking. "Can't disappear in a flash of blue, either. I smell her here, though. Strong."

Mika scrambled down to the side of the rocky alcove, avoiding the drop. "Can you repeat all that? I've caught most of it."

I placed the heels of my palms on the moist needles, and recited most of what I'd said with some clarification. Phistrel and Olivia joined us before we finished.

"Any of you ever heard of anything like this?" Mika asked the team.

Phistrel shrugged. "Aligns with random bigfoot lore. If I didn't know, I'd think it was that."

"Dagen smells werewolf," said Olivia. I couldn't tell from her tone whether she argued against my recall, or simply commented.

"Never smelled a bigfoot or a yeti." Dagen's tone hinted at humor, but her face remained grim.

I shifted as Mika crouched beside me and spoke. "We'll

need to send an official report to the Consociation once we get back within range of a signal. Someone might have data to let us know what we're dealing with. That's later. For the moment, how are you physically?"

To show my fitness, I rolled to my knees and pushed up with a minimal amount of grunting and wincing. I stretched, forcing the grimace to appear like a smile. "Just dandy."

"You can walk." Mika didn't ask a question. "Problem is getting you down to where Olivia saw a road, and then a twenty-minute hike back. Phistrel, you're with me. We're going for the car. Olivia, Dagen, get Kristen down to the road."

Before anyone left, I grasped white Haven, and the elusive muddy Earth realms, and mixed them as I washed it over my body. The same vibrations came from the spell as it had while working on Leah. Some aches intensified before they eased; all of it took more of my dwindling energy.

Phistrel watched intently. "I'd heard," he whispered. Then he cleared his throat. "I've heard you can work with the Earth realm. Does that heal?"

"As much as I can manage at the moment," I replied. "I'm hoping I'll be less likely to break my neck going downhill." In truth, my body begged for sleep, right here on the forest floor.

Mika and Phistrel left while Dagen paced, sniffing the alcove one last time. Olivia hovered near me, but watched the others climb down a subtler slope heading west.

"There's going to be quite a stir over this," she said.

I frowned. "The other cryptid?"

"I'd have to ask a Merfolk or a dwarf for the last time the Consociation identified a new cryptid. Most of those have come from Tarus."

Dagen snorted. "Not from Tarus. Probably from Ya Keya. That's why it smells like a werewolf. You ready?"

What she said made some sense. I shambled toward the slope where Mika and Phistrel had disappeared, drawing concerned looks from both Olivia and Dagen.

Olivia spoke. "If you start to fall, I will grab you. I apologize ahead of time." She respected that I'd see the Tarus realm upon contact.

"Thanks. No need to apologize. I've worked with David for quite a while."

The walk to the road paled in comparison to the sharp angle I'd fallen down. I moved from tree to tree, maintaining my balance unaided. By the time we reached flat dirt, I had enough ease from my aches that I turned north at an ambling pace. The quicker I could sit in a cushioned chair and drink some water, the better. A change of clothes was in order as well. I kept shaking out mud and needles as we walked.

"We've got about thirty-six hours before we'll be overrun with Mer biologists and researchers." Olivia's sharp, snapping scans of the surrounding woods continued, though Dagen would have mentioned any fresh scent of the werewolf — or bigfoot.

"Might even bring a dragon-shifter, unless they already know about these long-haired werewolves and haven't deigned to tell us about it." Dagen's voice carried a bit of the bitter respect that most held for the dragon-shifters.

I could imagine that someone had spotted the cryptid or blue flash at some point in history. The massive database Tomas kept might contain something. I'd check, someday. "What does that mean — it is following the werewolf?" I asked.

Olivia settled the issue of what to call the creature. "Let's name it bigfoot, for now. You raise an interesting question. Why risk being noticed over our werewolf? I'd gather they are elusive, since there's folklore attached, but no Consociation acknowledgment."

"Is it hunting it? Helping it?" I avoided mentioning any implication of the demon in front of Dagen. "It has to be tracking it. Dagen would have identified its presence at a scene, right?"

She grunted an agreement, letting me and Olivia banter the question back and forth without coming close to a motive for our bigfoot.

When Phistrel and Mika drove toward us, kicking up dust, I was glad to take the conversation into the Ford because I was thirsty and tired.

"We're going to drop you off at your car so you can head back and change," Mika informed me.

"Thank you."

"Neddie's map is getting updated, so we should get together after you pick up Leah from the airport. Does that work? I know we're messing up your time with your daughter."

I'd already dug that hole. "We'll meet after I pick up Leah."

"During that time, Pyre wants you to check in."

My energy sagging, I nodded and slid down in the chair to finish the bottle of cool water. Olivia reignited the same conversation with Mika, and I felt little purpose to rehash it. Maybe they would come up with something new. I missed Tomas and his encyclopedic knowledge. The bumps of the rough road disappeared as my thoughts drifted.

I woke when we stopped at my car. One of them might have called my name, but I started and straightened in my seat to recognize my rental. "Sorry, I fell asleep."

"We noticed." Dagen chuckled.

My aches relegated themselves to a scrape on one wrist and the entirety of my back. I stepped out, stiff and groggy. "I'll call you when I have Leah." I'd need to get her flight details to track the plane.

The heat had built up in the Subaru, warmer than the air outside, so once I had the engine running, I rolled down the window. I checked my phone, connected it to the car, and dialed Jade.

After it rang for a minute, I left her a voicemail. "Heading back to the site. Hope to see you." She might be busy, or she didn't want to talk.

I plugged the campground into navigation before dialing Marie. She answered immediately. "I'd like to hear this from you," she said in her usual businesslike tone.

My explanation had become rote after the third time, and I tried to be clear but concise for her. The only time I veered was near the end. "Is there anything like this in the archives?"

"Bigfoot, sasquatch, or yeti lore is a relatively recent development over the past few centuries. The blue flashes are rare in documentation. Nothing has ever been confirmed by the Consociation, but essays exist suggesting a connection to Ya Keya." Marie's tone lightened. "I've had a refresher course from Tomas."

Finn's distant voice chimed in. "I think you've impressed him."

For some reason, that made me smile. "Anyway, Dagen confirmed it to be the same scent she'd identified as a female werewolf. What we can't figure out is motive."

"Keep on it. First order of business is to stop the killings. That part of Montana will soon be a hotspot for Consociation biologists. Leah should be there ahead of them."

"Can you have Finn text me her flight details?"

"Tomas sent them to your email."

"Good enough. How's the case?"

"Cold as winter's edge. We're planning on packing up tonight, unless these next interviews lead to anything."

"Sorry to hear. I'll try to get a chance to read the reports."

"I'll be looking forward to your report soon." Her tone had reverted to an order at the end.

At the turn onto the paved road that I easily recognized, I turned right for the market rather than heading directly to the campground. The navigation began yelling about alternative routes.

"Sounds like you're lost. Check in with me once you've got something new." Marie hung up.

I needed coffee. My body wanted food, and I gave serious thought to waiting for a pizza to cook. My mind ached for sleep. Settling for cheese puffs, I snacked on them on the way to the campground while still trying to puzzle out our bigfoot's motives.

The gas station near Swan Lake finally looked open. It had been closed so often that I'd thought it was shut down. Through the trees behind the building, you could see the water. I'd have to stop in at some point, but for now I continued down the road, curving south toward the campground.

At the left turn into the campground, a young woman gripped her barking dog by the collar, waiting to cross to the lakefront. Most of the sites had filled with RVs and campers since I'd arrived, and most were quiet except for one boisterous drinking group of middle-aged men parked around a fire. They offered a gregarious greeting as I passed.

I had a couple hours before I'd have to drive to the

airport. A smile spread when I imagined bright Leah joining us.

My lips tightened as I drove toward our site, and I brushed streaks of orange cheese dust onto my jacket.

Jade sat alone and waiting for me at the table. Her eyes turned to mine as I pulled in.

CHAPTER
FOURTEEN

I steeled myself, unsure whether Jade would vent her displeasure or hide it. The distant murmur of sounds in the campground and forest intruded after I turned off the Subaru and climbed out. Faint wisps of smoke from the fire pit wafted the aroma of burgers into the air.

"Hey, honey." I stepped to the trunk to retrieve my purse.

The Turners' truck in the drive told me they sat inside their fifth wheel, perhaps to give us time to talk.

Black hair, straightened from the swim, shifted as Jade watched me. She'd changed into a long tee with a hint of shorts showing. Her eyes didn't sparkle with anger, but neither did they smile.

Jade waited for me to close the trunk before she asked a question. "What happened?"

"There was another death," I said, in preparation to tell a story that I could, without exposing anything the Consociation would frown upon.

"No. Your clothes." A sharper tone conflicted with concern, showing her underlying emotions.

"Oh, I slipped. We were in the woods. You know how clumsy I can be."

She snorted, blinking, then she focused on the table. "How long are you here for?"

"I have to pick up Leah a little after three this afternoon." I gestured to the tent. "Obviously, I need to change." With coffee and purse in hand, I headed to her table.

"They came by the site, mentioning there had been bear attacks."

"Who?" I asked.

Jade gave a quick shrug. "Someone from the campground, I guess." She nudged her head toward the Turner's camper. "They're talking about going into Kalispell this evening. Meghan's mom wants to leave."

I took a minute to sip my coffee, waiting for her to continue. When she didn't, I asked, "What's in Kalispell?"

"Some museum, shopping, ice cream." She didn't sound enthused. "Is it dangerous, whatever it is?"

"Very."

"You'd want me to leave?" She brought her gaze to mine.

"Yes, because it scares me."

She lowered her voice. "I haven't had any visions."

"Honey, we know that isn't the way it works. They're not reliable."

"The last one I had was about the cave." She turned to glance at the mountain range. "Are there caves around here?"

"I imagine." My coffee had grown cool, so I finished it while digging through my memory of our conversation where she'd told me about her vision. I chilled. "The hairy creature eating something at the cave, right?"

"Yes."

"Can you describe it?"

Her eyes widened, and she clasped her hands together, rubbing her thumb as if nervous. "That's what you're investigating?"

My lips twisted. "You know I can't say. Please."

"Okay, dark shaggy hair."

"How long?"

"Three or four inches. Big, I think. Taller than you. It knelt over something, but had a piece in its hands that it brought to its face. I only saw it from the back." She shivered. "I don't want to leave. Meghan and I have been looking forward to this for so long." Jade swallowed. "I wanted you to be here."

"How about I suggest that you leave with the Turners and go to a different park, maybe in Oregon? If we finish here in time, I'll meet you there."

"I thought you had to fly back Tuesday."

I smiled, raising an eyebrow. "They owe me, eh? We'll try to make this work out, honey."

For the first time in our conversation, Jade's lips twitched close to a smile. She nodded and stood to give me a hug. "I'm sorry," she whispered.

"Nothing to be sorry about. This whole business is messing with our trip."

When she released me, she brushed off her hands. "You should change."

"Agreed."

Jade pulled a long pine needle out of my hair. "Maybe a quick rinse, too."

I grimaced. "Am I that bad?"

"Oh, yeah." A real grin spread across her face, and my heart wanted to burst. "I'll see you inside." She headed for the door of the Turners' fifth wheel, still wiping her hands.

If I'd been in better shape, I'd have skipped to the tent,

instead of plodding like a worn plow horse. I'd brought a change of clothes for each day, so I grabbed Saturday's and left my purse.

The Turners were playing Yahtzee with Meghan when I entered, and Cheryl's eyes widened. "Are you okay?"

"My middle name is not Grace." I chuckled. "I'm fine. My jeans are another matter. Mind if I grab a shower?"

"I'd wonder if you didn't." Cheryl glanced at her family. "Are you working on the bear situation? We've heard about it all over."

"Yes. I'm sorry it's gotten in the way."

"No. No, I didn't mean it in that way." Cheryl swallowed. "How dangerous is it?"

"It's very dangerous. Jade had mentioned you were thinking of leaving?"

Harry frowned. "Uh, there's bears, um, up here. We knew that coming."

Cheryl ignored him, eyes focused on me with a mother's expectation.

"True. However, you know from Oregon that we rarely have any deaths related to them. Never in the summer. This one is different. I'd suggest taking the warning."

He fussed with his nose and lips, still not relenting. "Why do they have you helping? Uh, are you out hunting it?"

I smiled and shook my head. "The FBI has resources and connections to the FWP that are useful. I'm just facilitating and coordinating with the locals, that's all. No hunting."

Harry nodded quickly, but appeared ready to stumble through another comment. Cheryl still waited.

With a wave toward the window with a view of the forest, I continued. "While you've got something dangerous out there, the locals will keep the trails closed. It would be best to just move to another a campground in different area." My expression remained pleasant, but my thoughts were more realistic. *If not, I'll be calling my ex to get Jade out of here.*

Cheryl took the cue and brought out her phone. "Let me look at some parks, dear. The girls really wanted to hike."

"Uh, I suppose. It'll mean losing a day's rate for canceling." He rolled a die under his finger.

"I bet you could negotiate that," I said, "considering the circumstance."

"Oh, I will," grumbled Cheryl.

I glanced at Jade, who straightened. "Yeah, I'd like to go hiking."

"Yeah, Dad. You promised." Meghan joined in, and Harry sagged.

Well played, honey.

As I climbed into the small bathroom, Cheryl rattled off options. Though I hated losing my time with Jade, I breathed a sigh of relief. If she were safe elsewhere, it'd free up some of my concern and guilt.

I dug pine needles and other assorted items from my hair before checking for ticks everywhere. When I turned off the water, I ended up scraping the debris from the drain lest I leave it for Cheryl. My body still ached in spots, but I couldn't imagine expending the energy to heal it further. What I wanted to do was lie down and sleep, but if Jade and the Turners were leaving, then I should spend some time with her before picking up Leah.

As I changed in the small confines of the bathroom, I noticed a message from Finn. REPORT?

I snorted and offered a rude finger to my cracked screen, then typed, SOON. PROMISE.

When I walked out with my bundle of nasty clothes, I

saw that Jade had joined the Yahtzee game. "You want to play, Mom?"

"Sure, let me dump these in the tent." *Soon is relative, Finn*, I thought.

While we played Yahtzee, I apologized and mentally sketched a report on bigfoot between my turns. Jade and Meghan had a heated competition going, so she barely noted my distraction. I wasn't the only one, as Cheryl spent her time trying to track down a site for tonight.

She finally sighed, pointing her screen at Harry. "Three hours away. Trails and swimming. Electric and water."

"Uh, that looks fine, um, fire pit?"

"Yes. Problem is it's occupied until tomorrow afternoon check in."

Harry brightened. "I'd prefer to drive in the morning. We can still visit the, uh, museum in — Kalispell."

I stopped writing my report, looked up, and opened my mouth to speak, but Cheryl spoke before I could. "It's season. Everything is booked within a hundred miles. You two can sleep inside with us."

"I'd really rather it be tonight," I said, though knew that the only chance of that would be to have my ex, Anthony, retrieve Jade, ending the trip for her.

"So would I," she countered.

Jade studied me with a deadpan expression that included flat lips. I'd slipped past her disappointment with me into some form of acceptance and reconciliation that would vaporize if I ended this trip for her. As horrible as it was to take into consideration, the werewolf had just eaten and might be sated for the night.

I forced a smile for Jade. "Yes, I'd feel safer with her inside. Thank you." If the werewolf did sniff out a couple of witches, the aluminum door would do little to stop it. However, I'd have enough warning to prep a binding spell.

When Yahtzee ended, I bid the Turners and Jade goodbye to go pick up Leah.

"You'd love her," I told Jade. "I'll try to bring her by to visit." Leah didn't seem like the camping type.

I pulled out of the drive while they piled into the truck. Bugs had gotten in my open window, though the weather had never warmed up. People had fire pits ready for cooking as I drove through the campground. Maybe the locals would close the campground once they'd considered the two deaths.

My stop at the market on the way to the airport confirmed my status as a regular, at least temporarily.

"Just brewed a pot," the man at the counter said.

My phone dinged as I thanked him. Mika had sent a link to the map with a note that it had been updated. They were doing checks on the witches Neddie hadn't been able to reach. So far, everyone was alive. Either the werewolf had just passed the potential targets on his route south, or we had the motive wrong.

I texted Mika.

IS THERE ANY OTHER CONNECTION TO THE VICTIMS, OTHER THAN BEING WITCHES? WERE THEY IN THE SAME COVEN?

NO TO BOTH. NEDDIE'S BEEN SEARCHING TO SEE IF THEY'VE HAD ANY INTERACTION AT THEIR JOBS OR ON SOCIAL MEDIA. WE'VE TALKED TO THE THREE COVENS THEY BELONGED TO. NO CONNECTION THAT THEY KNEW. ON YOUR WAY TO THE AIRPORT?

YES. STOPPED FOR SOMETHING TO DRINK. I'LL CHECK IN AFTER I PICK LEAH UP.

I paused at the counter, enjoying the rich aroma of freshly brewed coffee while I flipped back to the map. With a mark that denoted an active witch residence, one dot stood south of the last location and very close to the campground.

Wʜᴀᴛ ɪs ᴛʜᴇ ᴘʟᴀɴ ꜰᴏʀ ᴛᴏɴɪɢʜᴛ?

Wᴇ'ʟʟ ᴛᴀʟᴋ. Dᴀɢᴇɴ ᴡᴀɴᴛs ᴛᴏ ᴛʀʏ ᴅʀɪᴠɪɴɢ ᴀʀᴏᴜɴᴅ ᴡɪᴛʜ ʜᴇʀ ʜᴇᴀᴅ ᴏᴜᴛ ᴛʜᴇ ᴡɪɴᴅᴏᴡ.

My chuckle brought a glance from another customer, so I tucked away my phone and poured fresh coffee.

When I pulled into the parking lot of the small terminal, I'd finished the best cup I'd had on this trip. With time to burn, I sat reviewing reports and messages, including Marie's comments on my report.

I still didn't feel like we had a solid grip on this case. Too many pieces didn't fit. Perhaps speaking with Leah would help.

When she texted that she'd landed early, I jumped up and scrambled inside. The terminal, as when I'd landed, didn't have a lot of people. Even the thin stream of passengers disembarking didn't change the sense of emptiness.

Blonde hair bobbing, Leah strode quickly out of the exit with a bright pink roller bag. Beside her, a short man with a thinning bald spot nearly jogged to keep up, chatting at her with a smile. She wore a silver chain under her pink and lavender blouse with a black skirt. Her blue eyes, highlighted by dark eye shadow, locked on mine, and a broad smile widened her round face.

She waved in exaggerated arcs. "Hey babe!"

Her companion gave me a surprised glance, but veered with her when she turned in my direction. Leah waited until she stopped in front of me to turn to him, patting his head on the bald spot. "It's been a pleasure, Michael. Bye."

His eyebrows dropped. "Darren."

"Goodbye, Darren." Leah hooked her arm in my elbow, turning us away from him. "Shall we?"

FIFTEEN

As I walked across the small terminal, Leah's arm crooked in my elbow and her pink case clattering behind us, I asked, "Darren?"

"Sat next to me and spent the entire trip talking. I fell asleep twice and woke to a dissertation on sheep grazing once, and a rant on the dangers of illegal immigrants the second time. I do *try* to be nice." Leah snorted. "I almost started growing hair over my lip to see his reaction."

I chuckled. "I would have enjoyed that."

"So, man-eating werewolf, and — something else."

"Yep. Hanging out with my kid."

"Yeah, what are you doing about that?"

"I think they're leaving, but not until tomorrow." She released my arm as I moved to open and hold the door.

We stepped out into the cloudy day, and Leah stopped to take a deep breath. "That is some clean mountain air." She closed her eyes, nostrils flaring. "Even better than where Pyre's working."

"Tough case?" I asked.

"Not really, just dead leads. In the middle of a gig, band members start swinging, and the whole crowd dives into a redneck mosh pit. No one had a good reason why."

My step faltered as a thought wedged into my brain. "Anything like Jojo's?" Our cold case, my cold case, had eerie similarities. "Beetles?"

Leah laughed. "No. Finn and Pyre talked about it, but dismissed it."

"Fatalities?" We reached my rental, and I unlocked the trunk.

"No. Locals have arrested five people on aggravated battery. The Consociation hasn't found enough cause to interfere."

We stowed her bag with my purse, and I pulled out my phone to check in with Mika. I dialed, set it to speaker, and laid it on the console as I started the car.

"Hey. Leah make it?"

"With bells on," Leah replied.

"Hey, girl." Mika's tone turned sultry.

Leah laughed. "Stop it. I'm here on business. What's the plan?"

"We're going to camp out at what might be a next target."

"Camp?" Leah's eyebrows rose. "Tomas booked me a room. Shower. Bed. Amenities."

I drove the Subaru across the parking lot toward the exit. "Is that the marker down by my campground?"

"Yes. Probably can't pull up the map at the moment, but it's the closest point to the last victim for twenty miles, unless the werewolf doubles back." Mika paused, then dropped their voice. "In your opinion, would a newly turned rogue werewolf have a direction or course?"

Leah glanced at me before responding. "Well, as rare

as it has ever been for a Biera to lose someone newly turned, they've never acted with any discernible purpose, beyond hunting."

"Right. Good to know. So, our target is about four miles from Gary Atkins's place. Distance and timing are irregular, but that is the distance between our first scene and Gary's, so our present target would fall into range."

I slowed to a stop, quickly bringing up Neddie's map on my phone before handing it to Leah. "When you say camp out at the target, do you mean for two days?"

"If needed. Dagen hates the idea." Mika spoke louder, perhaps needling Dagen.

I hated the idea that the target was so close to the campground. "What if it changes patterns? Are we sure it hasn't attacked in addition to the scenes we know about?"

"We've been busy clearing Neddie's list. I think we're up to 95 percent on the confirmations. The last stragglers are closer to the hikers than along the route south."

Leah scrolled on my cell. "Red is for victims. What's orange and light orange?"

"Orange are witches' locations, or were. Phistrel has convinced the covens to help persuade the witches to relocate, at least for tonight. Pale orange is unverified," Mika replied.

Leah frowned. "Attacking witches makes no sense. They are more able to defend themselves than mundanes."

"Yet here we are." Mika sighed. "Our encounter with it has left Kristen believing there's a demon involved."

I rolled my grip on the steering wheel. "I've never felt panic like that before. We've handled worse out of Atlanta."

Leah tilted her head in agreement, still scrolling Neddie's map. "I read the report. Fear is an indicator of demons. Some feed off it."

"As you said, why attack witches who could defend themselves, unless they were disabled with panic." I pressed my point, more for Mika than Leah.

"Great argument, Kristen. Let's discuss when you get here. You've got the address on Neddie's map. Bye."

We drove for a few minutes in silence as Leah studied Neddie's map. "So, I've never heard of a demon possessing a werewolf."

"Me neither. Dagen says it is unusually strong, and that's common in possession."

"Hmm. It looks like Tomas booked me near the stake-out. Not that he knew."

"You never know with him." I spoke with a cheery tone, but I felt like she'd dismissed my concept of a demon, much as the others had.

Early in my career, I'd learned to keep my harebrained ideas to myself, then when they'd led me to a lead detective position in Grand Junction, I'd relied on them. Marie had kept me from reverting to my newbie behavior that protected me from ridicule, and now I wrestled with my reactions. I wouldn't dismiss the possibility of a demon, but remain open-minded about it.

"Have you met Everek?" I asked.

Her smile told me she had. "Quite a character. Likes cars, though I haven't figured out how he sees over the dash."

We kept the chatter light, off the present situation, while she told me stories about her occasional cases in the west with Mika and the team. When we reached the gas station by Swan Lake, I pulled in to top off and grab something to drink. The sharp scent of the store's coffee pot had me choosing a chilled vanilla latte.

While I pumped the gas with Leah leaned against the car, a black pickup roared up. With the gun rack full, I wasn't surprised to see both men jump out in camo, down to their boots.

"Ladies." The closest had stained teeth and chewed as he eyed us over. "How's the gas?"

"Delicious," said Leah without a pause. "Five-star."

"Ha, quick little lady, eh?" He grinned when he shouldn't.

"Faster than you think." Leah offered a charming smile, then took another sip of blue Gatorade.

He paused for a moment, then continued to chew and tipped his camo hat.

I waited until they both headed for the store before speaking. "I bet they're here to hunt the bear."

She frowned, then nodded. "Got it. Well, good luck."

"They'd get shredded."

"Didn't say who I was wishing luck to."

A few minutes after leaving the gas station, we reached the turn down a dirt driveway where Mika's team had parked in front of a plain-looking house. There were no other cars. Dagen walked across the field that served as a lawn, veering to intercept us.

Leah rolled her window down. "Someone needs a nap."

Dagen smiled. "Can't. Kristen fill you in?" She leaned on the frame of the window, head tucked to peer over to me.

"We had time. Saw some yokels ready to go poke the bear." Leah shooed Dagen back to get out, and I opened my door.

As I rounded the hood, they hugged in what appeared a squeezing contest. "Is the witch here?" I gestured to the house. "Who is it?"

"He's gone. Mika pulled the Consociation business card, and he couldn't pack fast enough, promising not to breathe a word." Dagen grinned. "That first handshake never gets old. You'd think they never met a werewolf."

"Some haven't," I said.

Dagen scanned the woods. "Wish they'd sent David too. He's a riot."

"That's one word." Leah offered the comment in her droll voice. "Fill me in. I've heard Kristen's version."

I leaned on the hood while Dagen gave a recount of the case, even animating the skirmish. The sun leaned toward the west, but wouldn't set for hours, leaving the house without shade. If we were going to set a proper trap, we'd need plenty of wards for the windows and doors. *Maybe leave the door open, like Gary's.* At the thought of a poor raccoon tangled up in a binding, I giggled.

Dagen, explaining my slide down the embankment, laughed. "You were a sight, flailing about and kicking up pine needles. Glad you got them out of your hair. I kept mistaking you for a porcupine."

I patted my hair, finally dry from the shower. "Hilarious."

She shrugged. "It was, if you think about it."

Leah clapped Dagen on the shoulder. "So, sleeping in the living room tonight?"

"I doubt I'll sleep. Phistrel will set up the wards Kristen suggested."

"I'll be dreaming of you from the comfort of my hotel room, or whatever the lodge is. I hope it doesn't have a bunch of drunk hunters."

Dagen raised an eyebrow. "Talk to Mika about that. I think they and Pyre have other plans."

Leah grew serious. "Crap. I'm still checking in. I wish David was with us. He'd be miserable." She pointed to the house. "Let's hear their plan."

I followed, curious as well.

When we were five feet from the door, Mika burst out, bringing us to a halt. "Wonderful. Leah, lovely to see you. Back in the car with Kristen. We've had a sighting."

SIXTEEN

I drove while Leah connected with Mika via text, getting us the details of the sighting. After we passed the campground, the lake opened up to our left in an expanse of rich blue hemmed in by dark green hills. The clouds had cleared to a paler gray.

"Shit," Leah swore as we pulled behind a line of ten cars braking in front of Phistrel. A truck coming the opposite way blocked our view for a moment.

Exhaust blew in my open window, but I tilted out to spot the knot of sheriff's vehicles pulled to the side of two pickups. "I can see Rebekah and Buckley with the deputies."

As we slowed to a stop, a car door slammed, then Dagen popped out of her side. Mika and Dagen crossed the asphalt and trotted toward the congestion.

"I can wait," said Leah, though she rolled down her window, scanning the rock embankment to our right. She shifted her head, sniffing at the air.

We inched forward with a delivery van on my tail so close I couldn't see the driver in my rearview. Traffic had stopped coming from the opposite direction, so I leaned out farther. I made out a tow truck. "Did they mention an accident?" I asked.

"Nope."

The sheriff's deputies and the two pickups had pulled off the road onto a lookout that rarely had any visitors from what I'd seen. There were plenty of places along the lake to walk on the shore, including across from the campground. We were barely a mile away from the site. I didn't appreciate a sighting so close.

Mika had reached Buckley, but Dagen had disappeared. Rebekah waved down the line of traffic toward us before a young deputy began walking along the opposite lane. He spoke to annoyed people leaning out of their cars, but kept at a fast pace until he stood at the car ahead of Phistrel, then motioned us to move forward. I cringed, driving behind with an apologetic wince. One man had exited his vehicle to glare at us as we passed.

Leah waved liked a passing dignitary, deepening the man's scowl. "It's not Dagen that I smell, but the werewolf is female."

"That would be bigfoot."

I followed the deputy's directions, pulling tight behind Phistrel and hoping the rear of my rental didn't hang in the road. Leah popped out of the car as I put it into park.

When I exited and looked over my Subaru, I found the reason for the delay. A tow truck tugged at a pickup that had pulled off the asphalt on the opposite side, where there was no swale. One front tire rested on the rock embankment and the other on gravel, leaving the vehicle's back end tilted into traffic.

With her small pink purse strapped over her shoulder, Leah wove through the deputies, heading for Dagen, who walked on the side past the tow truck. Olivia moved to join me.

She pointed up the near cliff scattered with trees to a ridge three stories high. "Hunter saw it up there, did a U-turn, and parked there."

"How did they get up?" I asked.

"Don't know that the person who called it in saw." She motioned to the other pickups blocked in by the sheriff's vehicles. "They might be hunters too. Neddie's running plates."

"Dagen catch a whiff of our killer?"

"No. Just the bigfoot. She's trying to see if she can pick anything else up."

"Why come here? View of the lake?" I had thought that bigfoot hunted our werewolf. Now, I couldn't be sure.

Buckley shouted, drawing our attention. "You two take care of it, then. Feds." We turned as he grumbled something to the deputy nearest him, and they moved off to their vehicles.

Mika and Phistrel stood by Rebekah and a solid man with thin hair. He wore a beige long-sleeved shirt, a dark green vest, and a holster. "Who's that?" I asked Olivia, nudging my chin toward him.

"FWP warden named Chris. Didn't give a last name."

We stayed behind the Subaru as Buckley cursed and backed his sheriff's SUV out into the lane, heading south. I wouldn't miss him. Two others of his team had piled into their vehicle, waiting for him to clear. Four, including Rebekah, remained to deal with the traffic.

"Do you think they'll close the recreation areas?" Even if the Turners just drove to the nearest rest stop in the south, I'd be more comfortable.

Olivia cocked her head in a shrug. "I'm guessing we'll find out soon enough."

I peered at Warden Chris as he listened to Mika. At first glance, he didn't seem like a jerk, but you never knew. "Want to go listen?"

The other deputies had backed out, turning to follow Buckley. Rebekah leaned on the lead car in the northbound lane, chatting with the driver.

"Yes. We might be up for a hike, depending on Dagen's report."

As we walked, I gazed down the road where Leah and Dagen were continuing north at a good clip. The tow truck driver had exited to hook up the hunter's pickup properly after pulling it to the road.

We ambled up as Mika spoke. "The fewer people out there, the better. Maybe stick to helicopters?"

Chris gave us a quick glance. "I can try. Truth is, most are up north with some of our people. They're combing the area around the residence of Gary Atkins."

"This could be reported as a false sighting," suggested Mika, "while you get something up in the air."

He nodded, turning to greet me and Olivia. "Good afternoon, agents."

Mika gestured to us in turn. "Agents Winters and Nordstrom. Chris is one of the game wardens local to the county. They found our two dead hikers."

He sighed. "The hunters marked them on GPS before they got word and moved south. We're getting a team out to recover the bodies. It's sad." He drew in a deep breath. "I'm thankful for your help, but still confused why the FBI is here. Not my call, and I'm not complaining. Agent Mika says you'll be searching this south area, so that will free up some of our efforts. We're spread thin, but we've got help arriving tonight from Great Falls, Missoula, and Butte. I'd really like some actual pictures, so we know what bear we're dealing with."

I pointed down the line of cars. "If you're going to dissuade the hunters from this area, here comes an option to get a message out."

A tall reporter jogged toward us, followed by a squatter man laden with a camera and microphone on his shoulder.

Chris forced a weary smile. "You're not wrong; thanks."

The tow truck driver had secured the pickup and headed for his door as he called out something to the nearest deputy. I stepped farther back into the turnoff of the lookout area, as traffic should begin moving. What I had assumed was a quiet highway had backed up quickly.

"Excuse me for a minute?" Chris asked Mika, as he pointed toward the reporter with one hand.

As a group, we pulled back while the warden intercepted. Mika studied us each.

"Why here?" I asked. "If bigfoot is hunting the werewolf, why doesn't Dagen pick up the scent of the male werewolf? Are we mistaken?"

"Phistrel wondered the same. This might be a bust, except we got a liaison with the warden. He's reasonable. Actually listens."

We paused as Rebekah walked backward to us, motioning for the northbound cars to proceed behind the tow truck. There had to be thirty vehicles.

"Got water in the back," she yelled to us over her shoulder. Still encouraging the traffic with one hand, she pointed to the sheriff's SUV in front of the Ford that Phistrel had parked. "Did Chris mention the hikers?"

"He did," Mika said while typing. "I'm checking in with my agent now to see if we can get him up there. Any word on what the hunters saw?"

Rebekah checked with the other deputies, and they began waving on southbound traffic, locking us into the lookout. "When we find them, we'll be asking. Our call came from a real estate agent out of Missoula who says she saw a brown, could be black, shape dart into the trees before the hunters slammed on their brakes and nearly killed her. She thinks they're hunting black bear."

She turned to face us. "Water anyone?"

I nodded and moved for her vehicle. One pickup that I had assumed belonged to hunters bore official logos on the dark gray side. Chris had stopped the reporter and cameraman about ten yards away, positioning them tight against the traffic so the rocky embankment made the backdrop.

"You were vague about the other report. You sent it just before this. 'Nut job with drone footage. Will review.' Any more details?" Mika asked.

Rebekah laughed. "You asked me if I'd heard anything, even outlandish. Well, we've got a bigfoot hunter who lives out north of where the hikers parked. You passed his drive on the way up there. He sends us drone footage every month. His 'proof' is usually bears, so I brought it up when all this hit the fan."

With an armload of cold water bottles, I returned, offering her one.

She took it and continued. "There'd been a fire, so he sends his drone out toward the smoke someplace east on Bear Creek. Must had rain, 'cause it never turned into anything."

We waited, opening our waters as she sipped hers. "Now, he picks up the smoke and all, then for less than a second you can see what is clearly a wolf on the trail before it hightails into the woods. Not a bear, not bigfoot, just a lone wolf." Rebekah raised her bottle in a salute.

"Well, I asked for outlandish, right?" Mika snorted.

"Tell you what, send it to me anyway. I don't want my boss to think I ignored any evidence, no matter how irrelevant."

Rebecca pointed her bottle toward her car. "I can get you from here. Give me a sec." Mirth gilded her tone as she called over her shoulder, "Just the one, or do you want a year's worth?"

With an intense expression, Mika responded with an incongruous laugh. "Just the one."

"I wonder when and where," I whispered. "A fire?" *How did that fit?*

"Neddie should be able to get us a location from the footage." Mika glanced up from their ready cell phone. "Ready for a hike with Olivia?"

I frowned. "This afternoon?"

Phistrel watched Rebekah over my shoulder, speaking low. "We crossed over Bear Creek on the way up to the abandoned car. Neddie will have something by the time you get up there. Maybe fifteen minutes."

Mika flicked a smile at me. "Leah and Dagen will drive around trying to catch a scent. You'll be back to watch the house with me and Phistrel before dinner."

"You want me to sniff it out, see if there was a werewolf?" Leah asked.

"Yes, please."

I was already hungry, despite the cheese puffs from earlier. My energy still sagged, and the idea of a hike did not sound like fun. "I should have brought more clothes."

SEVENTEEN

Before we even left the lookout area, I called ahead and ordered a cheese pizza. "We can share," I offered to Leah.

"I'm good. I'll grab something to drink when we're there." Leah scrolled through her phone. I didn't realize she was reviewing reports until she started asking questions. "This panic that you and Phistrel experienced, wasn't it disabling?"

We'd just curved past the gas station that always seemed empty. "Not fully, but I had to fight to keep my wits. I reacted more than expected."

"Hmm. Your reactions are quick. Maybe these victims were caught off guard, though I can't imagine Paul Bates wasn't alerted after walking down those stairs. He'd have heard his door smashed open. That is what would have woken him and brought him down."

I ran the scenario in my head, agreeing with her. I'd have had a spell ready in each hand. "The werewolf was fast. Perhaps he missed."

"Or the terror was too much at that last minute. Both maybe." Leah tapped her lip and focused on her screen.

The trees cast shadows into the road from the sun dallying in the west. Traffic had picked up as people headed home from work, but it paled compared to Atlanta. I turned off our route to the familiar gas station and convenience store, ready to try their pizza.

With a last-minute decision, I pulled up to the pumps to top off. The potential threat to Jade had my maternal instincts getting everything ready in case. "I'll meet you inside," I said to Leah.

You're procrastinating, I told myself. My pizza wouldn't be ready yet, anyway.

The sharp scent of gas cut the otherwise pleasant air of Montana. A white Prius was parked on the other side of the pumps, with the owner absent. As I pumped, I stared at the surrounding mountains with most of my thoughts on the hike. We'd get directions soon, before we ranged up into the area beyond coverage, or there'd be no point.

When I went inside, I headed straight for the bathroom rather than check on my food. Leah opened one of the cooler doors. "Neddie sent the map to me, if you were looking for it."

"Good." My cell was in the car. I hadn't planned on checking until we were ready to drive, and I intended to have at least one hot slice.

Ten minutes later, I held two slices sandwiched together over a layer of napkins in my lap while I drove. The aroma beat the stale french fries, and the flavor rivaled the pizza closest to my apartment in Atlanta.

"Tomas confirms there's no documented possession of a werewolf by a demon in any archives." Leah slouched in the passenger seat, ignoring the bag of beverages and snacks she'd bought in favor of her phone. "You did your detection spells, I'm guessing."

"Yes. Phistrel too."

Leah sighed, perhaps putting the potential demon to rest as she tucked her cell away. We drove into the mountains through thick pines with driveways or other roads branching off. It was hard to tell the difference. I paused as the paved road ended, intersecting with options.

"Straight ahead, four-tenths of a mile. Then pull off to the side. We've got half a mile of hiking east of the road."

I checked the mileage to measure the remaining drive. "Did Neddie send you the video as well?"

"Nope. You bring bear spray?"

My eyes widened, and Leah laughed. She held up her hand, extending her black nails out an inch.

"Seriously. I'd like not to tackle an actual bear with your bare hands and my binding spells. Did you bring your gun?"

Leah jabbed a thumb toward the back of my rental. "In my roller. We won't need it. We've handled worse."

My lips pursed as I checked the dash. "Almost there."

The dirt road had a wide grassy swale on each side, with plenty of options to park. I slowed down and pulled to the left, grimacing as my tires crunched over twigs and weeds brushed underneath.

Before I exited the Subaru, I grabbed another slice of warm pizza and closed the box tight. I did not intend to spend half the case starving, like usual.

As I might have expected, my first step out of the car gathered a spread of stuck seeds from last fall's dried grass. Shade darkened the woods to the east, but the air had the rich scent of spring growth, even though the temperature hadn't reached sixty.

Pink purse over her shoulder, Leah plowed ahead of

me, pointing right to a trickling brook. "That's Bear Creek. The map shows it running up to the origin of the smoke."

"So, we might not get lost." I trudged behind her. "Slope's not too bad."

"Yeah, that will change."

My eyes grew accustomed to the shaded woods of dark browns and darker greens, speared with the occasional sunbeam through the canopy. Birds called from around us, and somewhere in the distance, a squirrel chattered. Leah kept pace ahead of me, easing up when I fell behind. We followed what might have been a path or game trail, though not well used this early in the season.

The incline steepened consistently until it forced me to lean into the walk, grabbing trees and branches for support. To the right, leaves crashed as something dashed away. I'd reached for Dur-Alf before recognizing the deer's shape.

"I can smell it," Leah said.

"The deer?" I asked.

"Well, yes, but I meant the smoke. Worse. Dead flesh. It's been rotting for a while."

I tensed, unsure what I'd expected from this trip. Leah was to come up here and sniff around. I was just the driver and support if something went badly. "Do you suppose it's an earlier kill?"

"Yes." She continued in silence for a couple more steps. "It might be human."

"Maybe another hiker. Where's their car?"

"We passed plenty of driveways less than a mile away."

As a kid, I'd trekked into the woods often, but rarely as an adult. The thought twisted my stomach.

Rocks broke through the grassy bank of the thin stream, making us wind about them.

"Seems like half a mile, doesn't it?"

Leah raised her wrist and shook it. "Forgot my Fitbit."

In ten minutes, we reached a point where I caught the scent of old smoke. The hill to our left sharply steepened and often broke with rocks that jutted through the forest floor. Trees worked around the obstacles, persevering.

Unseen birds flapped from uphill, so I lifted my gaze from my feet to the clearing, bright gold from sunshine. On the far side, blackened rock held darker shadows. The chilly air had me shiver.

"See it?" asked Leah.

I could have answered with what I saw, but prompted her. My breath labored. "What?"

"The corpse."

Then, no. I peered about, eventually focusing on the darkened rock. What might have once been doors lay charred on the ground. In front of them rested a corpse. I had a bitter moment of relief, as it appeared larger than any child. Blood-soaked bones piled in the remains of tattered clothing. Much of it had been picked clean, or the werewolf had been hungry enough for more than just innards.

As we reached the edge of the trees, I peered up to find the vultures circling higher. We'd disturbed their meal. The stench grew with each step.

"I don't smell werewolf, but it might have faded." Leah turned back to me.

"The drone picked up a wolf," I said. After our climb, my lungs craved air, waging war with my nose that wanted to stop inhaling.

The doors had been fixed to a square opening in the rock. All along the lip, the wooden frame had burned to char. The sun shone on a black floor before the darkness inside swallowed it.

Leah continued forward, so I followed, regretting the pizza filling my stomach. "Nice threads," she said. "Not hiking shoes."

"That's an old mine. Why would he be up here?" Before she could answer, I added, "Is it possible he died from the fire, maybe smoke or gas? An actual wolf could have smelled him."

"His clothes aren't singed. He might have started the fire, though. I doubt the werewolf did." Leah snorted, leaning down and tugging at the man's slacks.

When the bones slid, I coughed, rather than gagged. Dark, rotted flesh, hidden by the hips before, housed a nest of maggots that spilled and wriggled.

She used both hands to pull a wallet from the tattered rags, then rubbed it off in the grass. I moved to the side, upwind, and pressed my sleeve to my nose.

Leah opened it. "Mr. Pete Wright. Address in Kalispell."

"So, where is his car?" I asked.

"A good question." She poked through the contents.

"So Pete Wright comes all the way from Kalispell to light a mine on fire?"

I stepped on the closest burned door with care, and it shifted. My second footstep brought a dull snap as it gave way. I pulled my cell out and turned on the flashlight to peer inside. Smoke had blackened the walls and floor. Charred supports glinted under my light.

"We going in?" asked Leah. She strode over the remains and turned on her phone's flashlight.

A glance at the black that had likely been ancient wood to start with told me that we shouldn't, but I followed. By the time I reached the first burned arch, the reek of the fire replaced the stench of the corpse. I pulled a shield from

Dur-Alf as I passed underneath, but didn't deploy the spell.

Leah followed close behind with slow, careful footsteps that crunched on the floor. "Kerosene," she said.

"That's what started this?"

"Yes."

"Good, not gas from the mine."

"Would have warned you."

We reached a room with burned debris littering the floor and a sooty stone counter in the center. Glass and metal glittered under our lights. Charred shelves dangled from a wall.

I wiped at the soot, exposing the surface of the smooth stone table. "An altar."

"What was Pete up to?" Leah asked.

"Arcane magic. Pete Wright came from Kalispell to summon a demon. The same one that is working with the werewolf."

"Fits your theory neatly."

My lips twisted near to a pout. "Why was he here then?"

"Summoning something, or attempting some old ritual. Demon is a possibility. Maybe a love spell, as well."

I scoffed. "Doesn't exist. Nothing real anyway."

"Not all arcane users know that."

"You're right. It does fit though, somewhat." Not really. A demon could not control a werewolf; we'd hashed this out. An arcane user could summon one, but then what? Something had killed Pete Wright; either smoke or werewolf appeared to be the best options. "The lack of a car could mean someone else, a survivor."

"Nice. I like witnesses."

I shone my light to an opening at the rear. Five feet in,

rubble blocked any access, and my focus shifted to the rock above us. "Probably should get back and report this."

"A smarter idea than coming in." She smiled when I turned to her. "But we learned something valuable. I think it's connected to our case, don't you?"

"Yeah. I just wish one part of all this fit together."

EIGHTEEN

"Who do you suppose owns this property?" I asked as we left the gruesome scene. The vultures soared above the reek of the corpse, waiting for us to leave.

"Maybe the victim's partner, if he had one." Leah walked two paces ahead of me, navigating the steep slope with ease.

I proceeded with conscious care, not wanting to repeat my earlier slide. The pitch wasn't as bad, but I wasn't that graceful. "You don't build an altar in someone else's mine. Either Pete Wright, a family member, or someone involved will be connected to this land."

The sun had dropped farther in the west so that spikes of sun stabbed through the canopy, catching me in the eyes. Head down, I focused on my feet.

Leah stopped, coming close to having me bowl her over. Her head swiveled to our left, toward the thin creek. "Men," she said.

To my ears, I heard only birds and my foot shifting on the forest floor. I certainly couldn't smell anyone. "Where?"

"They are coming this way. I'd like not to get shot —" she smiled at me over her shoulder "— even if you can heal me."

I pulled a shield from Dur-Alf and placed it between us and the river. "I've put a shield between us."

She repositioned herself behind a trunk and leaned against it with her back and a heel. I'd have been halfway down the hill attempting that. "They'll be visible soon," Leah said in a bored tone.

Hunters could be dangerous if they spotted something moving. Many were responsible, but others drank or shot at the slightest motion without confirming their target. A killer bear might have some on edge, so waiting until they identified us made sense.

Shapes moved in the shadows, and we remained in place. Between the trunks and taller brush, glimpses of two men in camo with orange vests came more frequently. They walked in silence, peering about. One had a gray goatee, and the younger had a bushy black beard. Leah wore pink, and they still reacted by pulling up their weapons when they finally spotted us.

"Oh," the older man said before he lowered his muzzle and moved a hand toward his companion.

They were twenty yards away, close enough for us to read their expressions.

"What are you doing out here?" bellowed the younger man.

Leah rose off her tree. "Mushroom hunting. Good luck." She continued on our trek for the vehicle.

"Hey, wait." The man in beard called to us in a sharp, demanding tone.

I watched as the older man said something too quiet to hear, as if placating the other hunter. A moment passed, and I stepped to follow Leah.

The younger man couldn't restrain himself. "It's dangerous out here."

Leah chuckled and spoke low enough that only I could hear. "You have no idea, kid."

We reached the car after six in the afternoon, with the trees casting long shadows across the asphalt. The temperature threatened to drop. I glanced at the pizza box, then grimaced as the image of the man at the mine intruded. Luckily, I had some water left.

While we were still on the dirt road, Leah got a signal to her phone and called Mika on speaker.

"Hey, we got a body at a mine. Pete Wright from his ID. Mostly bones at this point."

"Was it killed by the werewolf?"

"I'd give it a high probability, but it's been rotting for a while. Everything has been at it. The mine was torched. Might have been an accident, no way for us to tell."

"What kind of mine?" Mika asked.

"Old, with an altar. I'm guessing that you'll find he was an arcane practitioner."

Mika remained silent for a few seconds, perhaps sending a message to Neddie. "What else do you have?"

"His license has him out of Kalispell, but there was no car. Can you find out who owns the property?"

"Felicia Howard. She lives in Missoula and is eighty-five with one son, Russell, and two cousins. I'll have Neddie track them all down. You think one of them might be involved?"

"Someone built the altar. I suppose Mr. Wright could have, but doubt it." Leah glanced over, as if offering me a chance to chime in. She had it handled. "Mind if I have Kristen bring me by the lodge to check in? We can meet you at the house in about thirty."

"Sounds good. See if they've got a restaurant."

"They do. Tomas plans ahead."

"He does." Mika chuckled. "I'll call in some orders. If they have steaks, rare?"

"You know me." Leah raised her eyebrows at me.

"Kristen?"

I nodded my head toward my cold pizza. "I've got pizza."

"Fries, baked potato?"

My lips twisted. "Okay, baked potato. Everything."

A half an hour later, it was taking longer than we expected for the food, so I stood on a rustic front porch with fragrant geranium baskets, calling Jade.

"Hey, honey. I have no idea how late I'll be." We'd never heard all of Mika's plan, and I didn't want to get her hopes up. "I'll make sure to see you before you leave."

"There were rangers in the campground this afternoon, suggesting people leave. Meghan's mom is happy we're leaving." Jade lowered her voice. "Is it bad?"

"Yes. I'm grateful you'll be somewhere safe."

She let the conversation drop into silence, and I frowned, wondering where her thoughts had taken her. "Can't you come with us?" Her tone was concern, not selfishness.

I tugged at my hair and swallowed. "Not yet, honey."

When we arrived back at the house Mika hoped the werewolf would target, Dagen jogged over to help with the bags for dinner. The simple interior of the house sported a small dining table where I sat with Olivia, while everyone else found seats in the living room on the sectional couch in front of the large screen. The aroma of steak dominated the room.

Mika ate sparingly, talking between bites. "We can't rely on the werewolf taking the bait. Dagen and Leah need to patrol tonight to see if they can catch wind of him. Kristen, are you okay with them taking your rental?"

The rental company wouldn't be, but the Consociation would handle any damage or difficulty. "Sure. I would like to see Jade before she leaves tomorrow morning."

"After we eat. Can you be back before it gets too dark?"

"Sure." The sun had been close to the hills in the west; I might have an hour or so.

"Great. Phistrel will set up a couple wards inside the front door." Mika turned to him, waiting as he swallowed.

"I'll mark the areas with a pink sheet for Olivia, Dagen, and Leah. Blue is safe. Don't use the back door. Assume outside any window will be warded. Upstairs and down." He gestured as he spoke. The living room had three windows, and the front door entered near the right corner.

Mika patted the couch. "Phistrel and Kristen can sleep on these. Neither Olivia nor I need much more than a chair."

Phistrel poked at his meal. "You just want the bait to be at the front of the house."

"Pretty much. We don't know how the werewolf senses witches." Mika checked everyone on the team. "Questions or concerns?"

Dagen spoke through a mouthful. "If Leah and I pick up a scent, you want us to call you, that's it."

"I told you, don't chase it unless we can plan some traps. You call, we come, unless it is close."

Olivia's sharp eyes flicked to mine. "What considerations have we made for any demonic influence?"

I was grateful that she asked.

"Since we haven't been able to identify the exact nature of its involvement, there is little we can do, except to be aware that we may have to deal with it as well." Mika raised both hands in a shrug. "The same goes for the bigfoot we found. My first focus is on the werewolf, since he's the one killing humans."

The house subdued to the sound of the team eating. I finished my potato. "What about the owners of the mine — any word?"

"Yes. I had Neddie send it to your email, but the son, Russell Howard, lives on the property that extends to the mine. I didn't send the locals out to the residence, but Neddie says there hasn't been any activity on the man's internet or phone in over a week. We'll check the house tomorrow."

Olivia turned to me. "He's fifty-one and on our arcane practitioner list."

"Leah," I asked, "if there had been a second body nearby, would you have caught scent of it?"

"I doubt it. Distinct scents blur after the body decomposes. I might have noticed two distinct species, but not two humans." She smiled. "We can head back with real flashlights if you'd like to check."

I stood. "Well, I've got to be back in time to be bait."

CHAPTER

NINETEEN

As I drove out to head for the nearby campground, the sun dipped into the western hills. Traffic had thinned to a single semi behind me. I rolled up the windows against the cooling air. The Subaru smelled like the leftover pizza now, and that suited me just fine.

Dogs barked at the entrance to the campground. A number of the first sites had been vacated, except, of course, the rowdy drunks who had a bonfire going.

The Turners had outside lights shining on the picnic table where they and my daughter were in the middle of a board game. All of them turned with smiles when I pulled in. *Can't stay*, I thought, though I wanted to.

Jade stood and ran over to give me a hug as I exited. "I'm glad you're okay." Her voice trembled.

My heart skipped, but I hugged her tight. "Vision?"

She nodded against my shoulder. "It was awful. You were against a gray wall, like concrete. I couldn't see what was holding you, but you couldn't get away. The building was dark. Huge. Someone else was screaming, and I think you wanted to help them."

I shivered. The house we were in had simple painted drywall, not gray concrete. "We know your vision might not be for now. That might be another day."

Jade pulled her head back, still holding me close, to search my eyes. "That doesn't make it any better."

It didn't.

Her ability as a seer came from an unconscious touch of the realms. Technically, we swam through them, but required thought and practice to activate them. Jade's brushes with Mer were the most accepted theory, though no one had solid answers. I considered her earlier vision of the hairy creature eating in the dark, and wondered if it was a bigfoot, not a werewolf.

"Um, you want some wine? Beer?" called Harry.

Jade wiped her face on my shoulder, forcing a smile as she let me go. We'd been silent for a couple of minutes. The dogs barked again.

"I can't," I said, edging a regretful tone into my voice. "I just came to see you off, since I won't be here in the morning."

Cheryl sounded incredulous. "They have you working tonight?"

Two gunshots snapped nearby.

Birds complained and rose from the trees behind the fifth wheel. The gunfire had been a double tap from one gun. As I spun to search around us, a second, lighter set of cracks strung out in a less controlled spurt. The first gun rejoined with three more shots.

"Inside." I pushed Jade toward the Turners and spoke loud enough for all of them. "Inside." The aluminum walls were little cover from bullets or werewolves, but if I had to use magic, I'd prefer they weren't watching.

The weapon fire stopped.

I faced southeast where the activity had come from.

Dark trees hid all but a pair of flickering lights. Clouds hung low, with a sharp contrast of deep gray crevices and bottoms lit by the setting sun. The silhouettes of birds swung in low arcs. I could see well enough, but not very far through the vegetation.

The door to the camper creaked, and Cheryl's hushed voice issued quick commands. I eased when the door clicked shut. Pulling two detection spells from Haven, I tossed them deep into the woods, but nothing bigger than a rabbit waited there.

My phone buzzed in my pocket, startling me. Did I expect the werewolf to come crashing into the campsite?

Jade was a witch; untrained, because that would only amplify her visions and bring notice from the Consociation.

In whatever manner the werewolf detected his prey, would he consider Jade? *She needs to leave.* My hand shook as I pulled out my phone.

Mika called. "Did you hear gunfire?"

Stupidly, I nodded. "It was over here at the campground. Southeast corner."

"On our way." Mika hung up.

I stood in the cold listening for some hint of threatening activity, but only the unending barking and indistinct murmur of voices echoed in the woods. Somewhere in the area, an engine started. If they were smart, they'd be leaving.

Jade and Meghan watched me from the upper window of the camper. I flashed a smile, as if it might comfort them.

A siren sounded from the northwest. I'd prefer Rebekah over Buckley.

Mika arrived first, jumping out of the SUV before it continued past our campsite. "Anything?"

"I lit up detection spells, but nothing came close. We forgot about my daughter. She has some skills that might attract our werewolf tonight."

"Really?" Mika's eyebrows rose as they glanced at the fifth wheel. "I never saw that in the records. Are they leaving?"

"Morning."

"Want me to have a word?"

"Sure." I'd rather Jade be safely away from here, though it hurt to lose our time.

Mika strode up to the camper. In their dark suit and shiny black hair, they had the professional air about them that Marie demanded of us.

After three knocks, Cheryl answered the door. "Did you catch it? Is it safe?"

"It is not. We're going to be helping the FWP clear the campground now." Mika showed their FBI badge.

Cheryl turned to me, then back to Mika. "Why are the FBI involved?"

"Interagency cooperation, ma'am. We've got resources the FWP doesn't. We're sorry for the inconvenience."

"That's okay." Cheryl appeared relieved. "We'll get ready." She closed the door, and her muffled voice sounded from inside.

Mika strode to my car, dialing, then speaking into the phone sharply. "Anything?"

I couldn't hear the muffled response.

Harry stepped out. "Um, should we leave the tent?"

I almost chuckled. "Oh, no. I wouldn't get to enjoy it." With a quick check on Mika, I headed for the tent. "Let me get my stuff out."

The next fifteen minutes became a scramble as the Turners, Jade, and I broke down the site while Mika moved to the road to talk in privacy. Jade tried to hold a smile, but failed consistently.

"I'm hoping this will be over quick enough for me to grab some time with you — before I have to go back to Atlanta." I knelt on an air mattress, helping deflate it.

"I understand. I do." Jade seemed reasonable at the moment, but I knew her teenage moods could swing.

As Harry broke down the tent, Mika met the SUV in the drive. The dark gray FWP pickup pulled up along the road. Olivia separated from the group and headed for me. Her eyes noted everyone's activity, as if cataloging it.

I moved to my car with a loose wad of dirty clothes and met her at my rental's trunk. "Was it him?"

Olivia shook her head. "Her."

"Not sure how I feel about that. We still don't know bigfoot's role in all this."

"I think she's searching for him."

We both paused as Harry jumped in his pickup and fired it up.

"Am I in the way?" I called to Cheryl, pointing at my Subaru.

She moved toward us with an appraising eye for Olivia. "If there's two things he's good at, it's driving and mixing drinks." Her eyes widened, and she touched my forearm. "Not that he does them at the same time."

"Good to hear. Cheryl, this is Agent Nordstrom."

"Pleasure to meet you." She shook Olivia's hand.

"Unfortunate circumstances." Olivia didn't attempt to smile.

I gestured to Harry as he backed the truck toward his fifth wheel. "Are you going to be all right driving tonight?"

"I found us a rest stop a couple of hours away. We'll crash there for the night."

Ten minutes later, I hugged Jade goodbye and, at her

request, promised to call her in the morning. Her mood might change, but we parted on a good note. It pleased me that Cheryl made the kids ride in the back seat of the truck, even though they whined. The sun painted the gray clouds with gold and orange.

They weren't the only vehicles I'd heard or seen drive by the site, likely on their way out. For Mika's team and me, the crisis had ended, but rumors of a man-eating bear and gunshots would weigh heavy on anyone who intended to stay the night. I'd rest easier knowing Jade would be far away.

As Olivia and I joined the others, Chris, the FWP warden, listened to Mika. "At least a site to site visit to recommend they leave. It'll be less of a burden for your people."

"I agree," he said, "but until I get a final order from command, we can't tell them to leave."

A rifle cracked close in the woods behind the site.

TWENTY

I paused a moment as Chris burst into a run in the direction of the second bark of a rifle. Mika and Dagen matched him stride for stride, with the rest of us steps behind.

"FWP," the warden yelled as he lit a flashlight into the dark shadows of the woods.

Meanwhile, I sent two Haven spells into the trees where Mika would see the effect and Chris wouldn't. A pair of running rabbits shot to the east, and birds lifted from the treetops. The effort drained me. I'd forgotten how much I'd used already.

"I don't smell any werewolf." Leah said in front of me.

Chris called out his warning again, but I could hear no response as we crashed through the underbrush.

Phistrel and I hit the trees at a fast jog, with our werewolf and vampire teammates able to dart around obstacles easier.

"Hunters?" I huffed out the question. The gunshots earlier would have attracted attention. I hoped that the light from the flashlight would identify us, as it didn't help my footing in the low bramble and weeds.

The trees thinned out, not quite a clearing, but perhaps one decades ago. Dagen stopped short, earning a curious glance back from Chris.

Leah caught up, head tilted up as if sniffing. "It's her and two men," she whispered.

Chris had slowed, but didn't stop, flicking the light back to Dagen. "What is it?"

Dagen caught Leah's eyes, nodded, then pursed her lips, jogging toward Chris at a less energetic pace. "Nothing, I thought I saw something."

"What?" Olivia asked Leah.

"The hunters passed through here, but bigfoot's scent begins and ends right here." Leah leaned down, sniffing.

I peered back the way we'd come. "I doubt we would have seen a blue flash from the campsite. Maybe she caught the hunters' attention, and they fired."

Leah opened her small pink purse to pull out a tissue. She wiped it over the pine needles. When she flipped it up, bright red streaked across the white. "They shot her. I don't think it's a heavy hit. I barely caught the scent."

Phistrel nodded. "Let's keep up."

As he and Olivia jogged ahead, Leah folded the napkin carefully and tucked it in an inside pouch of her purse. I imagined the Consociation would want to study it.

We spent the next half hour trailing behind Chris's flashlight until the darkness made my progress close to impossible. When the beam turned toward us, I sighed in relief and sagged against a nearby tree. "Have we been on the hunter's trail the whole time?" I asked Leah.

She gestured to the right. "They curved east a while back."

"Tell me we're not lost."

"Between all of us, I could follow that scent back through a rainstorm."

I was thirsty, and suddenly craving chocolate; something I avoided eating around Jade. "So, I'm guessing we're back to Mika's plan."

Olivia spoke as she studied Mika, Chris, and Dagen returning. "It's a solid plan, but if our werewolf keeps to his schedule, we won't have an active night."

"I could use some rest," I said.

"Gary was attacked in midday," added Phistrel. "How tight do we believe the timing is?"

Leah lowered her voice. "If it's just raging hunger, then I wouldn't count on a specific interval."

"So, do you think this is a newly turned werewolf?" I asked.

"It fits best."

Her agreement with Dagen brought mixed emotions from me. I'd prefer we had a clean idea of what to expect, and they both seemed to think the behavior predictable. However, Olivia and I had both discussed irregularities with the wine between feedings, the distinct southerly pattern, and the proclivity for witches. The demon fit in there somewhere.

When the others joined us, Chris surprised me. "Do you mind if we talk for a moment?" he asked.

"Me?" I squeaked.

Mika's head cocked. "Now?"

He considered the question. "It should only take a minute. However, it can wait if need be."

My thoughts reeled, trying to come up with any reason he'd have. I'd barely ever spoken in front of him. Did it have something to do with Jade?

"We'll wait," said Mika.

Chris looked at me, taking a second before he asked,

"Do *you* mind?" He sincerely requested my consent to speak, which set him apart from about 95 percent of most male enforcement officers that I'd ever met.

"Oh, yes. I mean no, I don't mind." He had me flustered.

He walked beside me into the forest until we were out of earshot, or would have been for humans. Chris leaned down, eyes peering out from under his brows to watch my reaction. "Are you all witches?"

My eyes widened. "I — no." The temperature had dropped with the sun, but I shivered as I considered my options for lying.

Chris tugged at Dur-Alf with the lightest touch, causing the mossy-green realm to ripple. "I'm not very talented," he said, "but I can see when Haven is used."

Mika, who would have seen Chris's display, called out, "Ah, introductions are in order."

Still a little stunned at the turn, I flushed from my initial attempt to lie to him. On rare occasions, I could sense what I thought was a witch, but didn't rely on it; some were more sensitive about it. Since he mentioned Haven, then he'd seen me through the detection spells, or at least guessed it was me.

"We all work for the Consociation," Mika stated more bluntly than I expected.

Chris nodded with a stiff movement to his body. "So, if you can tell me, what are we actually hunting, then?"

An impish smile touched the corners of Mika's lips. "Introductions first."

Dagen grinned, offering her hand. We all watched Chris's reaction. He did well. His eyes widened, but he didn't flinch or pull away.

Leah offered her hand like a noble who expected a kiss on the fingers. Chris swallowed, forcing a smile.

He blinked at a handshake from Mika. Merfolk were not common, at least around rural witches. Phistrel brought a curious gaze until he spoke. "Everyday witch, sorry." This brought a smile to Chris's dazed expression.

Whereas most had appeared to enjoy the reveal, Olivia shook his hand with a deadpan face. Chris spoke at last. "I had not realized that the Consociation was so — integrated."

Olivia replied, "It has changed over the past few decades."

He turned to Mika. "What are we up against?"

"I'll talk as we walk. It's chilly." Mika waited until Dagen and Leah took the lead, then strode behind them. "It's a werewolf. There's a high probability that it is newly turned before it went rogue."

I noted the lack of mention of any demonic activity, or of bigfoot, but Mika might get to it in time.

Chris offered a sheepish smile. "I'm not very versed in werewolf behavior. I apologize. It hadn't crossed my mind, though it might explain some of the autopsy irregularities. Also, the claw marks at one scene seemed far too small."

"We believe it is feeding every forty-eight hours or so." Still Mika did not mention any of our other findings or concerns.

He walked without responding, either considering the evidence or giving her time to continue. The rest of us remained quiet. I wanted to see how much she'd bring him in.

Our footsteps crunched a chaotic racket, with twigs snapping and branches brushing against us. It grew louder the longer the silence lasted.

"It's hunting witches while moving south. Where do you live?" Mika asked.

"Whitefish. On the lake."

"How far is that?"

"Forty miles north."

Mika grunted. "That's why you didn't come up in our search. We've been warning local witches out of the area."

Lights sparkled in the woods ahead from headlights, then disappeared. We were getting close to the campground.

"What can I do to help? I imagine you don't want these hunters anywhere near here."

"I don't. They won't have a chance. After tonight, it'll take something big to get them to ignore it." Mika's head cocked, studying Chris. "That, you could help with."

"Can you explain?" asked Chris.

"Willing to lie?"

"More than I did this afternoon?" His lips curled in jest.

"A lot more."

He paused, then hurriedly replied, as if realizing Mika expected a response. "Yes. It might save lives."

I appreciated his sureness, though we had a long way to go before we could relax. However, we all knew that, Chris included.

"Head up to one of the first victims about ten miles north. Fire off a few rounds. Call a couple of your other game wardens up to help. Let the deputies find out. The hunters will likely be tracking radios and hear the chatter. Stay up there. By morning, we should be clear down here."

It took us another fifteen minutes to reach the site. Leah and Dagen had us spot on target. Chris said quick goodbyes and headed off in his truck.

Twilight hung to the west, while stars had sprung up in the east. As a group, we watched him drive away.

"That worked out," I said.

"Do you have any idea the number of reports I'll have

to fill out now?" Mika asked me, their tone teasing. "I already pulled the Consociation badge out to evict witches, but him I had to tell about the werewolf."

The Consociation did not take lightly their exposure, or the DRC's, to any outside person or organization. With Marie, it had only happened while detaining a witch or arcane user, that I knew of, and they would have soon learned the truth, anyway.

"At least he's a witch." I rarely used magic in sight of mundanes, but it had happened more often lately with the DRC.

"Small fortune."

"It helped," I said. "He's off distracting the hunters."

"I would have had him doing that in any case. That was the plan once I realized Dagen had given up on anything beyond pretense. So what happened?"

"Bigfoot got shot," said Dagen. "Appeared, got shot, and disappeared."

"So we have hunters who saw the blue flash." Mika cocked their head in a shrug. "It's already lore, so not too big of a deal. I'll have Neddie keep an ear out to see what they gossip about."

Olivia gestured. "Leah got some of the bigfoot's blood."

"Excellent. I'll get Everek to come down and pick it up." Mika appeared pleased. "A new species, and we already have some potential data. When they show up tomorrow, we'll have a new circus to deal with."

I'd forgotten that Merfolk and Dwarves would want to learn about the bigfoot. "Do you think she's hurt bad? Leah said there wasn't a lot of blood." My question highlighted that I thought of her as an ally, not a threat.

Mika clapped my shoulder, bringing a flush of Mer. "First things first. Transfer whatever is necessary for the night out of your car into our rental. Give Dagen and Leah the keys."

I pulled my keys out, considering what I might need for a night or two on the couch. I'd sleep like a rock, especially after the futile chase with Chris. My hope remained that the bigfoot had not sustained a severe wound, but bullets weren't merciful.

When I loaded a bag and purse into the SUV, I did not forget the leftover pizza.

TWENTY-ONE

I returned to the simple house with Olivia carrying my bag and Phistrel pointing out the wards he'd placed from the threshold. The path into the room required hugging the front door to my right, then turning at the edge of the television.

"I don't expect anything tonight, so we'll take turns keeping watch. Two-hour shifts for the next ten hours," Mika explained.

Phistrel brought a cane-back chair from the dining area and placed it behind the wards, facing the door. "Plenty of coffee. Some diet soda." Our dinner had left a pleasant aroma to the air.

Olivia sat. "I've got the first shift." She watched as I sat on one leg of the couch, pulling out a cold slice of pizza. "Did you have any idea about the game warden?"

Mouth full, I shook my head.

With an armload of blankets, Phistrel returned from the other side of the house. He tossed one beside me.

With a crisp turn of her head, Olivia focused on the door. Her intensity made me wonder if I could sleep with her like that. After a glass of water and a trip to the bathroom, however, I found I had zero trouble crashing.

I woke to my phone ringing and daylight bathing the trees outside. My feet caught in the blanket, and I nearly face-planted to answer Jade's call.

"Hi, Mom. I wanted to check on you."

"All's good, honey."

"Did I wake you?"

"No. Where are you?" As I asked my question, I scanned the room. Someone had brewed coffee, and the aroma should have awakened me.

Phistrel and Olivia sat at the dining table, listening to my conversation. Had someone taken my shift? I smiled at them.

"The new campsite." Jade's voice hinted at disappointment.

"Oh, good. How is it?" I rolled my shoulders; I'd need a shower, if possible. When I stood, I spotted Mika talking to Everek in the front yard. My curiosity rose.

"It's okay. There's a lot of people and not many trees."

"Sorry." I moved toward the kitchen area in my socks with the hope that the owner kept cream and sugar for his coffee. "Listen, I'll call you later today. Is that all right?"

"Okay." The disappointment in her voice hurt, but I was grateful she wanted to talk with me after all this.

"Promise, honey. Go have fun."

I hung up and foraged in the fridge, happy to find decent coffee creamer. "Are Leah and Dagen still out there?"

Olivia pointed a slender finger at the hall. "They're napping. They took turns during the night, but want an hour of solid sleep."

"What happened to my shift?"

She watched me steadily. "I took it. You used a lot of magic yesterday; I know how Phistrel gets after heavy use."

He leaned his head back. "If it makes you feel better, she took mine as well."

It did. "So, no sign of our werewolf?"

"No," Olivia answered.

"Everek?" I pointed with one hand to the front, pouring coffee with the other.

"Mika had him work with Leah and Dagen to get any blood he could find from the bigfoot where she'd been shot, after he checked out the mine area for any other bodies." Phistrel scratched at his beard, then stood. "No sign of Russell Howard. Mika wants to send you and Leah to his house when you're both ready."

"Good." I sipped at the coffee, pleased with the result. More so, I was grateful we'd had a calm night. If I headed over to this arcane user's house, that meant Phistrel got to stay here and act as bait. As much as I didn't like that idea, I'd rather we catch this werewolf and close the case.

An hour later, after a shower, a fresh set of jeans and a sweatshirt, a second cup of coffee, and a slice of cold pizza, I drove with Leah north to the residence of Russell Howard with my water bottle full. Saturday traffic at 7 a.m. was nonexistent except for semis.

Finn called as I pulled down a dirt drive leading to the man's property. "We're back at the office. How's all the hubbub over bigfoot going?"

I frowned. "We still haven't dealt with the werewolf."

"Yeah, Pyre said as much. I figured you'd be celebrity status at this point with questions about bigfoot."

"Haven't caught up with us yet," said Leah.

"Hey, Leah! Having fun?"

"Sleep would be fun. I spent the night driving around with Dagen."

Finn chuckled. "So, the Consociation geeks haven't caught up with you yet. What are you working on?"

I drove within sight of the residence and slowed to a stop as I answered. "We just arrived at someone's house who's name came up in our search for the ownership of the burned-out mine. They have a connection to the victim there, Pete Wright. I think I see his Honda Accord parked at the house."

"Be careful. Wards and all that. I'll let you go."

When I stepped out of my rental, I spun two detection spells to the sides of the house, covering some of the encroaching woods. Little more than birds and rabbits glowed.

The two-story building might have been a hundred years old, maintained well during a portion of that time, but the paint had faded, and edges of the roof sagged.

"License matches," I said to Leah, pointing at the Honda belonging to Pete Wright. "We were right on that part of the puzzle."

"The BMW wagon fits Russell's vehicle." It sat sideways to us, nose to the side of the house.

As we walked closer, I tugged at Dur-Alf and Mer, just to see if any wards had been placed along the walkway. A small, empty porch lay at the front door. Weeds sprouted green in dry shrubs along the outer walls. Blackout blinds covered the inside of every window. The home screamed, "Go away."

"Front or back?" asked Leah.

"Front. I'd detect if anyone was inside." I kept tugging at the realms, but no wards showed. I'd expected something from an arcane user. "Let me work on the door alone."

Leah waved me on. "Have at it. Normally we'd just send David blundering inside."

I chuckled, though it wasn't always true. With a shield from Dur-Alf pressed against the door, I stepped onto the porch to unlock it with Mer. "Not locked."

"Could be a rural thing."

"Maybe." I turned the knob with a lifting spell out of caution and eased the door open. It moved easily, then hung.

The shotgun blast made me jump as wood and pellets embedded into my shield. I stumbled backward until Leah's hand steadied my shoulder.

"Not very neighborly," she said.

With a jittery nod, I released my shield and the debris it held so we could peer through the remains of the door. A wood frame held the smoking weapon, but the barren room gave no hint of other furniture. I tugged on Dur-Alf, lighting eight wards that I could see. "I'm guessing he doesn't come in this way."

"Wards?" Leah asked.

"A few." We retreated and began a lap around the house, starting to the right. "Any scent?" I asked.

"Nope. No werewolf, no bigfoot."

Blasting wards marked the windows, even a trio of small ones in the back that might have given a glimpse into a basement, had they not been painted black. Most were drawn visible even to Leah, but a couple were invisible except when I tugged on Dur-Alf. The only other door waited on the west side where Russell's car was parked. A simple alarm ward had been sketched on the single step with charcoal.

I tugged at it through Dur-Alf until a thread broke and it deactivated. Leah let me lead with a shield as I picked the lock and lifted the door open with Mer. No shotgun greeted us from the small mudroom.

"Is that a trip wire?" asked Leah.

With my shield shifted to the doorway, I had just stepped up to the threshold, so I peered at my feet. "Where?"

She pointed at the far end of the mudroom to a low thread.

"Yep," I said, taking a step back. "Activate it?"

Her forehead wrinkled as she squinted. "Any wards?"

I checked. "Nothing within sight."

"Can you shield me from both sides?"

"To an extent."

When she moved forward, I pulled up a second shield and placed it inside with the first so she had a corridor. Why would an arcane user, capable enough to create wards, use a manual trap?

Leah stepped with care up to the trip wire, then leaned out, scanning the corners that I couldn't see. I winced when she stepped over and crouched to the left.

"Let me readjust the shields."

She waved me back. "It's just a grenade."

Just a grenade. "Okay."

The line went slack, and my breath hitched. Leah stood, beckoning me. I released the shields and took a deep breath, tugging at the realms with each step. The scent of spent gunpowder wafted in the air. Leah lit her flashlight, stabbing the beam across an empty but well-used dining table, then into a kitchen with immaculate and modern appliances.

A Russian grenade rested in a clamp beside the threshold of the mudroom. The door to the bathroom stood open, and the interior appeared as clean as the kitchen.

"Upstairs or down?" Leah had stepped toward the living room, where open stairs branched off from the hall: one up, one down.

I tugged at Dur-Alf, marking a ward on the first step to the basement. "Let me clear the ward, then downstairs."

She made way, and I tugged at a blasting ward with Dur-Alf, untying it. I pulled out my cell and turned on the flashlight.

"Let me go first," she said. "I've got better vision." The trip wire had proved that. "How far down can you check for wards?"

"There are no more on the steps or on the walls leading down."

She moved to the edge and took a tentative step down. A click sounded, but from above, not below. The lights in the basement lit, including one overhead.

My heart thudded back into beat.

"Camera." She pointed into the bright light.

With my hand up, I squinted until a small shape showed beside the flood lamp. "We should have someone check the internet here."

Leah continued her descent, and I kept checking for wards. The concrete floor remained clear of arcane markings and anything resembling the normal debris one expected.

Concreted blocks rose to form an empty wall lit by bare bright bulbs. No workbenches or shelves lined the sides, just gray concrete.

"Very clean," said Leah as she reached the bottom. "Russell Howard likes everything neat." She watched as I tugged at the realms, though she could not see the results. "Clear?"

I stood at the base of the stairs beside her, peering about the well-lit basement. The only openings were the windows at the back, painted black. "No wards anywhere."

She sniffed. "I've got his scent, a scent. He comes down

here as much as he is upstairs in his dining area." Leah crept, smelling the air.

I remained in place, remembering Jade's vision. How long would the lights remain on? Phone in hand, I watched her.

Leah made one complete circuit, circling the stairs in the center before returning to the wall opposite the base. She crouched, sniffing. "I think there's a door here." Her fingers traced along the blocks. "Yes. No mortar."

"Let me try." I checked the blocks where she'd touched and made out the empty spaces. With a shield between us and the wall, I first tried unlocking with Mer wriggling along the gap, then I formed a lifting spell and began tugging.

When something inside the wall clicked, the lights doused, and I flinched. Leah had left her flashlight on, so I blushed at my surprise and tugged. An irregular door of concrete blocks pulled forward with barely a grating sound. It stopped, so I wormed my lifting spell around the edges until it swung open with ease, stopping as it pointed into the room.

Neither of us moved forward, and I scrambled to tug at the realms, checking for wards, while Leah directed her light inside the opening.

TWENTY-TWO

When my phone rang, I dropped it on the concrete floor of Russell Howard's basement. "Crap."

The hidden room had a ceiling of wooden beams at the height of my forehead. Leah's light caught two steps leading down to a rock floor webbed with crevices. The door built of interlocking blocks jutted out at a ninety-degree angle. "Do you smell that?" she asked.

I crouched to retrieve my phone. The protector had fresh cracks in it. With a grimace, I declined Jade's call. "Musty?"

"Bones. Human bones."

"Lovely."

She edged forward, and I tugged at all the realms, craning to see if any wards waited on the floor or ceiling. Her flashlight caught the stained wooden legs of a workbench deep on the left. As she lowered her head and shoulders to enter, I crouched as well, fumbling to turn on my cell's flashlight.

Leah paused, one foot on the first step. "Someone has

been collecting ancestors, I would guess." Her flashlight pointed to the right.

When she descended to the second step, a sharp click echoed in the chamber, and she pitched forward as if the stone had given way.

I pulled a shield from Dur-Alf without a thought. As my hand moved to throw the spell in the room in front of Leah, the concrete block door swung into my side.

My cell hit the floor, but I wedged my shield between the lip of the door and the wall, pinning the trap open near the top.

Leah leaped out, brushing her head against my Dur-Alf magic, unseen by her. She grunted, settling her hair with one hand. "I'm really hating this jerk. Though I'm guessing he's dead somewhere out near the mines."

I already had an unlocking spell from Mer probing into the hinges. "Everek checked and didn't find anything."

"Dwarves have a lousy sense of smell." She cocked her head. "In comparison. Besides, the scent's old."

An unlocking spell is intuitive, and one most witches learn early on, along with lifting. Both require an extension of your will, though not with any genuine sense of touch. The spells explore, relaying the general shape and consistency, so I found the spring that pressured the door to close, but no way to release it. "I think it needs to shut before it can be unlocked, but I can't be sure."

Leah reached up and patted the air until she found my shield pinning the door open. "This will hold?"

It would strain my energy over time. "Yes."

She sighed and hopped into the room, ignoring the steps completely and digging out her phone.

I dismissed my unlocking spell, picked up my cell with its screen protector webbed with cracks, and entered with more caution as I stepped from the basement floor to the rock of the chamber almost two feet below. A long, empty workbench stretched along the north side. From above it hung a three-foot work lamp with a cord that I had no intention of pulling.

Corkboards plastered with paper clippings, drawings, and photographs covered the wall. The most interesting sketch depicted Akkadian sigils for Tarus, designated for demons. Through a maze of fractures on my screen, I managed to get my camera on and took pictures for Neddie and the team.

Leah's phone flashed behind me. "I'm guessing this is generational. Someone needs to have a long talk with Felicia Howard."

"I'd just like to get out of here first." When someone returned to study the chamber further, either I or Phistrel would need to help to get the door open and keep it open.

To the east, shelves had been carved into the rock, and ancient warbled glass doors sealed in jars and pots of ingredients with a section of grimoires. I wouldn't be touching anything. Leah joined me in taking photos of the items through the panes.

On the south side, four skeletons lay in vertical crypts about sixteen inches high, dug into the wall. The color of the bones had darkened. Russell Howard and his family wouldn't be the first witches to store ancestors, though few followed the practice nowadays.

I shrugged off the itching desire to leave and scanned the photos I'd taken. Despite the abuse of my phone on this trip, everything appeared clear. "We good?"

Leah frowned at my phone. "Did you just do that?"

"I've been working on it the whole trip."

"Hope that's just the screen protector." She made for the door, crouching lower than she needed to below my shield.

Once we were both clear, I prepared to release my shield, then thought better of it. "I'm going to wait until we're outside."

"Better safe." Leah marched for the stairs up to the first floor, and I followed on her heels.

I released the spell from outside, and the building did not explode. My desire to get back to the car and leave Russell Howard's bunker spurred my pace. The morning had warmed with no clouds in a bright blue sky. Thirsty and worn from using spells, I'd look forward to a more leisurely day if something new didn't pop up.

Leah dialed Mika as I started the car.

"Anything interesting?" Mika asked over the speaker.

"For a death trap? Not as much as you might expect. We got photos of his hidden sanctum. The front door is a bit of a mess. You do not want locals stepping inside." Leah clicked her seatbelt, glancing at me as if I might add a comment.

"He's got an interest in Tarus." I popped open my water bottle. "I've got pictures of the sigils relating to demons."

Mika remained silent, so Leah continued. "Pete Wright's vehicle is there, as was Russell's. I'm not sure we disabled all his traps."

"I'm messaging Chris to see if he can cordon it off without raising the notice of the other game wardens. I think most are corralling the hunters, but the house is just west of the interest area." Mika did sound distracted.

"Need to get someone to interview the landowner, Felicia Howard," Leah added. "They've got a small mausoleum in his sanctum. This is a family tradition."

We drove onto the paved section, which eased the jostling. Tall trees, at least sixty feet high, lined the road to form a shaded corridor that waited for the sun to rise higher. I sipped water, waiting for Mika to comment.

"Okay. Chris has a plan. You said pictures?" Mika finally asked.

Leah shifted screens. "Respond on the group email from Neddie?"

"That works. See you back here in a little bit."

"What's the plan for today?" Leah asked.

"Pretty much the same as last night. You and Dagen checking the area. The rest of us will man the target house. I wish we had something more proactive."

When we hung up with Mika, Leah took my fractured phone and sent bunker pictures to everyone. Traffic had increased since our arrival. While I would prefer to stop the werewolf and get back to spending time with Jade, a little rest sounded good. Russell's house had been a tense start to the day.

Leah's phone rang. "Miss us, Mika?"

Both of our cells dinged with messages.

"Meet us at the coordinates. There's been an attack."

It wouldn't have been at the house, or Mika would have said so. The bait hadn't worked. "Who?" I asked.

"Ginny Myers." A door closed in the background, and Mika continued louder. "Chris just got us the details. We're trying to keep the hunters out of the loop, but the local enforcement is not being helpful."

"Buckley," I said.

"Buckley. I've got to deal with that. Meet us there." Mika hung up as Leah pulled up the map on her phone.

"Hmm. Red Owl Trail. Isn't that where you all were attacked?"

I pulled onto the main highway where I'd spent most of my time and headed south. "That was the road. I doubt it is the same spot. Neddie has it marked on his map."

It took Leah a minute before she snorted. "Damn close."

Though I disliked doing so, I had to pass a truck towing a boat. "It can't be a witch unless they returned after we warned them away." I didn't like that our werewolf had changed his pattern. "How long until we get there?"

"Eleven minutes." Leah swapped screens, but I focused on the road, pushing over the speed limit. "Not a witch. Not really eaten either, according to the police report. Neighbors heard a disturbance, found the body on the side of the road, called locals."

"This is unusual. I wonder if we disturbed its pattern."

"By moving the witches out?"

"Maybe. It could also scent you and Dagen driving around."

"We would scent it as well."

True. I didn't like anomalies when we had such a clear pattern. In a few minutes, I passed the familiar junction that led to the gas station and convenience store where I'd frequented, then took the dirt road leading southwest. Bumpy; I had to slow down. The western mountains peeked through the forest, and I cracked open the window to let in the cool, fresh air.

By the time we arrived, seven sheriff's vehicles flashed red and blue along a stretch of the road. Mika's Ford and the warden's truck were parked on a winter-brown lawn behind them. Figures clustered there.

"We're here." I hadn't noticed Leah dial as I pulled off the road to park without blocking an empty sheriff's truck. She didn't put it on speaker. "Okay. Okay."

I grabbed my phone before jumping out and followed Leah up a drive congested with vehicles. She marched toward a house sitting about sixty yards from all the commotion by the road. Buckley, surrounded by six of his deputies, yelled at Chris. Rebekah smiled and waved as we pointedly avoided them, heading to the trees just north of the house.

"Chris is keeping them busy with the body." Leah nudged her chin toward the cluster. "The scent of both of them is strong."

"Both? Werewolf and bigfoot?" I asked.

She picked up her pace to nearly a run, forcing me to keep up. "Dagen's led Mika to those woods. They're waiting on us."

I glanced over my shoulder at Chris and the deputies. The angle afforded me a glimpse of a curving drive where we'd parked yesterday, below the tall pines. So close to the attack a day ago, but three miles north of where the werewolf had found a witch to target. It hadn't killed here before.

The location and the odd choice of a victim bothered me. "We need to be careful."

"Agreed." Leah's tone held a bite, not quite as excited as Dagen got when hunting, but sharper than her normal easygoing pitch.

We reached the edge of the trees, richly scented with the promise of growth and summer under the full sun. Leah wound through tall brush, some with bright new leaves. Shade darkened the undergrowth under the tall canopy, and I fought and stumbled, losing ground to her graceful speed.

I scanned the thick woods surrounding the back of the home, especially straight ahead where Leah led us. Four ghostly shapes formed from a Haven detection spell, though branches, trunks, and brush hid Mika's team from me. Besides, the spell faded in intensity over time, and the essence of Haven did little to identify more than general shape at this distance. From her restless pace, I guessed at Dagen a few yards from the cluster of others.

They clearly saw us, turning in unison. We were close to fifteen yards away, and my skin prickled as we drove deeper into the woods.

Leah had gained a distance ahead of me when I peered up at the canopy high overhead, and my step faltered. The Ponderosa Pine had grown thick near the top.

I tugged a detection spell from Haven and flung it upward over the team's heads. One turned their head up at my magic, either Phistrel or Mika.

A large ghostly shape formed as it dropped from the tops of the trees into the range of my detection, heading directly for the team.

TWENTY-THREE

As the werewolf dropped through the pine boughs, I yelled, "Overhead!"

My warning did little, if anything, and I might have distracted Phistrel as he pulled a spell from Dur-Alf. He'd been turned up to watch my Haven spell, and the mossy-green glow seemed to take too long before he activated it.

Mika and the rest of their team didn't react until the attacker dropped the last ten feet, but their response seemed to be cued by Phistrel's actions. The ghostly detection spell blended with what I could otherwise see through the brush. I swear I felt the thud through my shoes when the werewolf landed.

Phistrel launched into the air, and Dagen leaped into the fray. Leah broke into a run ahead of me, reminding me to do the same. My throat tightened, and I had to lean into my strides with weakening legs.

The figures danced and growled ahead as I recognized the terror building in my chest. *Not real.* It was. This werewolf ate people and had nearly bested us before.

Had Phistrel set wards? I panted for air as I rounded the low limbs of a young tree and the skirmish played out in front of me. With jerky, unsure movements, I pulled a shield and a binding from Dur-Alf.

Phistrel lay closest to me in a bed of needles, unmoving.

Mika had disappeared, a white figure under the Haven spell. Olivia, Dagen, and Leah surrounded the werewolf, darting in with punches and swipes.

As his furry paw swiped, blood sprayed from Dagen's shoulder, and the impact sent her sprawling backward, head over feet. Her shredded windbreaker fluttered like feathers.

I almost threw my binding spell, but Leah darted between us, raking at the werewolf's legs. Her bright purse was gone, and her pastel shirt sported dark wet spots.

My grinding dread spiked when the muzzle turned to me and widened. He stood nearly six feet tall, even hunched in a quasi-canine form. The sun caught his eyes, glinting red, as his maw appeared to smile.

With a sudden snap of a backhand, he caught Olivia mid-jump. The werewolf followed the flow of his movement and leaped to the side.

I took a chance with spinning my binding spell toward him from thirty feet away. Teeth clenched against the debilitating desire to flee, I pulled another from Dur-Alf.

My binding missed.

With an arc of three yards, Olivia slammed into Mika, toppling them both to the ground.

The werewolf pounced on Olivia, pressing her on top of Mika. Each massive cryptid arm took a turn to shred into their bodies, as his shoulders pivoted, then his head lowered into their tangled mass.

If I hadn't stopped mid-throw, I would have hit Leah

with a binding spell as she jumped on his back. From his quick spin, I wondered if he expected her attack.

Her body twirled as he reached back and grabbed her arm. His fur ribboned in her outstretched claws, but he showed impossible strength by not only ripping her off his back, but tossing her away like a towel.

Of the team, Mika and Olivia moved sluggishly, Phistrel not at all, and Dagen staggered to her feet.

The werewolf ignored them all and focused on me.

I stopped advancing, and my knees nearly dropped out from underneath me. *The panic isn't real.* My arm shook as I threw the binding spell.

Five yards away, he easily dodged my telegraphed pitch. His teeth were red with blood, and his claws kneaded the air at his sides. With a slow, deliberate step, his eyes locked on mine as if feasting on my terror like he would my flesh. A sharp, evil intelligence shone in his gaze.

When Dagen burst into a run for the werewolf, I dragged a fresh binding spell from Dur-Alf. My feet refused to move, though my heart pounded with the hope of fleeing. I would be easy prey. *Stand with your team.* Most of the team lay wounded on the floor of the forest. *He will kill us all.*

The werewolf launched to his right in a run on all paws toward Dagen. It pirouetted instead of a direct clash, but I couldn't summon any hope. My eyes flicked about, searching for some looming demon manipulating my emotions. They would show under the fading detection spell, but nothing lurked in the surrounding area.

Dagen screamed in rage and pain as the werewolf caught her ankle and whipped her toward Phistrel.

The werewolf spun toward me as the binding left my fingers. He dropped, letting the spell fling past overhead.

Needles flew into the air as he burst toward me on all fours.

Teeth clamped, I did not scream. With a flick, I barely managed to erect the shield a foot in front of me before he lunged and slammed into it.

I fell back, my legs finally betraying me.

The werewolf's muzzle turned to the side as it impacted, and it shrieked an angry growl.

While I flailed at Dur-Alf for another shield, he sprung away from the obstacle and darted around. I had to form the shield in a dome to the ground to survive his quick pounce. Dirt and needles flew from his rear legs as he landed atop my protection and tore at it with six-inch nails.

Shields usually give me some sense of comfort, but I felt none as I cowered, scrabbling for another shield spell. He would outlast me. In time, he would win.

His maw closed on the shield, trying to pierce it with sharp teeth. The panic had me panting, almost hyperventilating. *Fight it.*

If I could squeeze out a binding spell, I couldn't miss. The werewolf encompassed my shield so thoroughly that he blotted out the filtered light of the forest. My tomb darkened.

Claws dug at the sides of my shield and into the ground.

I couldn't control the trembling.

Suddenly, the werewolf turned away.

A shaggy body slammed into him, spilling furry forms over my dome. I shifted in the damp needles to get a better view.

Bigfoot swapped blows with the werewolf, who let out a rage-filled roar. When he tried to gain an advantage with his strength and grab at her elbow, she spun artfully out of his grasp.

He faced away from me. I wavered between dismissing my shield and launching a binding spell into his back, four feet away.

He caught her side in a quick swipe, and bigfoot howled. I thought she might be darting out of reach, but she bounded away.

The werewolf paused, flashing his eyes back to me, then tore after her with a throaty growl.

TWENTY-FOUR

The absence of terror washed over me, leaving me ashamed. I dismissed the shield and jerked to my feet. Bigfoot and the werewolf had disappeared into the underbrush and low limbs in a glimpse of motion heading to the west. With an abundance of caution, I wearily dragged a detection spell from Haven and tossed it twenty feet in their direction.

"Dagen?"

She knelt on one knee six yards away, with Phistrel still motionless behind her. "Gonna need a minute."

To my right a good distance, Olivia lay on her side watching me. "Where's Mika?" I asked. The white of Haven lit Olivia and should have done the same for Mika.

"Hurt. Mer," Olivia's voice slurred. I blinked, processing that Mika had left, gone back to Mer, leaving the team. When I took a step toward her, she pointed away. "Phistrel."

Leah sat cross-legged on the ground, shaking her head and gesturing toward him. I nodded, shuffling toward Dagen and Phistrel.

Dagen bled from her right arm. It dripped from the tatters of her sleeve onto the pine needles as I approached. "Let me help," I said.

She shook her head. "Phistrel first."

He appeared unconscious, which I might not be able to heal, so I ignored her. Pulling from Haven and Earth, I blended the healing spell as I crouched at her side. The strange sensation of melding washed over me, and her emotions of anger and guilt flickered. "I'm sorry," I said.

She huffed. "For what?"

"I was terrified." I had the vague sense of something in her body returning to form, not a renewal like I'd thought before.

With a wince, she gave me a dour glance. "You warned us. If Phistrel hadn't looked up, I wouldn't have."

Leah stood with a slow, deliberate push, then rolled her shoulders and back. "We need help." She scanned the ground, then plodded toward her purse.

"It was a trap, from the beginning," I said. The blood had slowed, and Dagen began working the cuff of her windbreaker back to expose the torn shirt sleeve below.

Angry red skin wove in a line from the back of her wrist across most of her forearm. "I'm thinking you're right. He's too strong. That was a bigfoot."

"Yeah. Well, we know they aren't working together," I tried to smile, but it came out in a weak frown.

"Why save us?" Dagen asked.

I didn't know.

Leah spoke from behind us. "Everek. Need an assist. I'm sending coordinates. Google maps, but it'll get you close."

When I stood, having done some healing on Dagen, my head spun. Olivia remained where she was on her side.

I shuffled to Phistrel, who lay face first in the pine needles. His body moved with slow breaths.

The forest about us had gone silent in comparison to the battle we'd nearly lost. Any hint of bigfoot or werewolf was beyond the distant shadows of the forest. My brows knitted. Why *had* bigfoot helped, and not just flashed blue to disappear?

With low energy, I knelt by Phistrel and blended realms to begin a healing. His dull, unconscious state clouded my own, or at least mixed with my weariness. I sensed aches, but little more. More time with someone training me would be helpful to understand this magic.

Phistrel jerked awake, both in my awareness and on the ground as he rolled over and spiked me with a binding spell.

On the wrong end of a spell that I often used, my focus blurred so that his quick thrash away took a second to recognize. His bearded face snapped in a frantic jumble.

"Phistrel!" Leah called from behind me.

In a split second, he untied the binding, and I lurched forward on freed muscles. "Damn," I sputtered.

"Sorry." Phistrel grabbed my upper arm, supporting me and keeping us from colliding. "I think my shoulder is dislocated, and my neck is pinched."

My balance restored, I forced myself to stand. Leah and Dagen were converging on us, both studying me and Phistrel. I gestured them to him, and stumbled toward Olivia. "How bad?" I asked her.

"Need blood." Olivia's ripped windbreaker hung loose on her shoulder, and the white shirt underneath had been torn to expose deep wounds on her chest and arm. Claws had sunk deep into her biceps. Her jaw had swelled from her neck to lips.

"Everek is bringing some," Leah called. She and Dagen crouched beside Phistrel.

"I'm going to try and stop the bleeding." Beside her, I dropped to my knees heavier than I expected.

She blinked and nodded. Her eyes appeared as sharp as ever, though she'd bled more than any human could survive. I dredged up Earth and Haven, promising myself to learn more than the little Herta had shown me. I needed to understand the magic, and she wasn't particularly chatty.

Stretching my hands wide, I held them over Olivia's shoulder, still uncomfortable around vampire blood. As with werewolves, I sensed the realm in her, but couldn't have been able to describe even how I knew it was Tarus. The healing balked and ebbed, draining me more than it had with Dagen. Olivia closed her eyes and pressed her lips tight.

"Does it hurt?" I asked.

She didn't answer, and I pushed forward. My vision darkened under the strain, and my ears pounded. If the werewolf returned right now, we wouldn't survive; I doubted any of us could put up a fight. We wouldn't leave each other.

Leah spoke somewhere nearby, but I couldn't quite make out her words. Phistrel, then Dagen, joined her. I heard his pained grunt, but couldn't process the meaning of it.

Olivia said something, but she sounded far away. Her voice repeated, sharper.

Someone yanked me backward, and I had no strength to resist. Earth and Haven slipped from my grasp, and the blue sky peeked through the treetops high above.

"Kristen?" Leah asked in a tight tone.

"Yes?"

"Are you okay?" My focus sharpened as I shifted to find her crouched behind my head. The soft bed of needles felt good to rest in.

"Yeah, tired."

"I think you overdid it, healing everyone."

She was probably right. We should be worrying about the werewolf. "I can set some binding wards."

Leah chuckled. "Phistrel, can you set a couple traps? Kristen is right to be concerned." Her face dropped over mine, blonde hair bobbing. "Take a quick rest. Everek is coming with someone. I can hear them."

"Mika?" I asked.

"It might be a few hours before we see them. Transitioning in Mer distorts time, but Mika will be back and healthy. Merfolk have it good in that way."

I closed my eyes. Somehow, I'd drained too much energy trying to heal Olivia. It might have been I'd run out of stamina, or vampires took more. "Olivia?"

"Better, thank you." Olivia spoke from somewhere at my feet. Her voice sounded clearer.

Leah stood, needles crunching under her boots and footsteps padding away as she moved to speak quietly with Dagen. We'd fallen for a trap that had nearly killed us. We were in rough shape. Mika would be gone for a while. In this state, we couldn't face a demon and a werewolf who worked together.

My phone rang. With thick, numb fingers, I fished in my pocket and dragged out my cell. *Jade.* "Hey, honey." I propped up on one elbow, then slumped back to the ground, ignoring the needles poking into my hair.

"You sound tired." She didn't mention me ignoring her call earlier.

"Busy morning." My cheerful voice sounded false.

"Sorry. I'm just worried. Have you caught it yet?"

It caught us, I thought. "Working on it."

Footsteps sounded in the woods, and I jerked to a sitting position. Everek, with his broad smile and cowboy hat, strode toward us laden with a cooler in one hand and a satchel in the other. A short dwarf with a red bandanna jogged beside him.

"If you can't get a hold of me, we're going on a hike. I didn't want you to worry."

"Thank you, honey. Text me when you get back. I don't know how busy it will be today. I love you." I'd expected to die less than twenty minutes ago, and felt some shame that she'd not been my first thought.

"I love you, mom."

Everek's companion scanned our group of shredded survivors, then pointed at me. "Is that her?" The voice sounded feminine.

"It is." Everek aimed straight for Olivia while his friend, untouched by any illusion, marched straight for me.

"I need a better description than long fur and decidedly non-canine features." The dwarf quoted sections of my report.

"Introductions," Everek called over his shoulder. "Niceties."

The dwarf had deep purple eyes and a white braid. "Yes. You're Kristen Winters and I'm Aili. Describe. Clarify. What was this mention of bigfoot? How can you assume a classification?"

Leah strode up, raising her eyebrows at me with a humorous tilt to her lips. "Well, aren't you in luck?"

Aili's head cocked. "How's that?"

"You just missed another sighting."

The dwarf pivoted to face Leah. "Did it attack?"

I rocked to my knees as Leah distracted Aili with descriptions that left out details of our situation. As tired as

I felt, sitting and waiting for another attack wouldn't help our predicament. We would need some help if we were going to outwit and overpower this werewolf. What we didn't need were Consociation researchers.

Olivia drank from a familiar pouch under Everek's ministrations. Dagen paced at the eastern edge of our battle grounds, where Phistrel had laid three visible wards and worked on a fourth. I fought the desire to rest and walked to him. His movements to form the ward were left-handed, though he flexed the fingers of the right as if testing them.

I kept my voice low. "Will Mika return here?"

He turned, exposing a bruise running down the left side of his face. "No. They'd know we'd be gone by the time they can return. It'll be at the house we've set up. That's the safest place they touched Mer."

Tomas had transitioned to Mer to heal. I had never asked much about it, but in all fairness, we'd been busy. What would the werewolf try next? The house where Phistrel and I were bait would probably be our best course — if the werewolf didn't return right here while we recovered from its last attack.

"Should we call Marie, ask for help?" I asked Phistrel. After all, half her team was here.

He considered it, lips tightening. "I'd rather Mika make that decision, but it might not be a bad idea. Ask Olivia, and if she agrees, make the call." Phistrel returned to casting another binding ward.

I glanced at Olivia and Everek, then trudged a wide arc around them, avoiding Aili and Leah's conversation.

Past Everek, metal glinted in a shaft of the morning sun. It took until I walked a few more paces to recognize it as a Glock. *Mika's?*

Olivia watched me as Everek wrapped her chest

wound; his illusion bent awkwardly at her side. The scent of bitter almond and a floral aroma hung in the air near them. As she drank blood to heal, her head turned to follow me.

"Mika's weapon?" I asked her as I picked it up.

"Yes. They are the only one on the team who carries a gun." Her words, thick and slow, had started to come more readily.

Mushroom caps poked through the needles at my feet. A fairy circle had begun, extending to encompass Olivia. Everek stood atop the edge. Some witches considered them important, though even my grandmother, Leyna, had never known why.

"Mer's kiss," Olivia explained.

My eyes widened. "Mika made this?"

Everek huffed. "I sure didn't. You'll know our doors when you see them."

I frowned, unsure whether he was jesting, though I knew Olivia wasn't. *So much I don't know.* I peered at the knobby caps, curious and exhausted.

With a tug from Dur-Alf, Everek pulled what appeared to be a type of shield spell.

My head whipped about, frantic that I might need to defend when I didn't have an ounce to give.

His laugh turned everyone's heads. "You've got the set of jitters, Kristen." With a snap, he formed a stiff shield on the ground in a familiar shape.

A stretcher. I flushed at my momentary panic, still feeling shame at the terror the demon had instilled in me. We'd been caught in a trap and bested, leaving us without Mika and Olivia. Somehow, there was a demon working with the werewolf, and they were kicking our asses.

"We should get out of here," Everek said. "Help me roll her onto the stretcher, and let's hike out."

I agreed, and knelt at Olivia's feet. We had too many unanswered questions, and I needed someplace to rest. "Oh," I said to Olivia, "what's your opinion on asking Pyre to come out to help? Phistrel said to check with you."

Olivia shifted, helping us get her on a stretcher she could not see. "We're outmatched at present, so, yes."

TWENTY-FIVE

As I lugged Everek's nearly empty cooler, Phistrel and Leah carried Olivia. The woods remained an eerie silence that had me checking the surrounding treetops.

Dagen led our troop, annoyed at the pestering dwarf, Aili. I didn't have the energy to deal with her.

"Your healing, while foolish, did well on her." Everek walked beside me, his illusion keeping up with our slow pace.

I assumed he referred to Olivia, as he hadn't even checked Dagen's arm. "You don't seem to have any bias about her condition."

"You refer to her abhorrent nature? She made the decision to destroy her own body. That choice should not affect the execution of my duties."

"Herta believes otherwise."

"Yes, she does. Do you miss her?"

I cocked my head toward the face his illusion wore in the hope he might hint at being serious. "I don't think she likes me."

"She is quite intrigued by you. We all are."

All dwarves, or just those who did healing? "Because I use the Earth realm?"

"Not that simple. You've learned to interlace two realms, and have an inherent intuition that you've displayed on werewolves and vampires that few have an aptitude for." He sounded serious, and if he were on the East Coast, I would have asked him to train me.

As the edge of the woods neared with brighter light and the hint of the house to our left, Aili drew from Mer the illusion of an elderly woman a foot taller than her almost four-foot height.

Everek snorted. "She does that so easily. Takes me half an hour."

I glanced at him. "You do make yours rather tall." In truth, I didn't know if it made a difference; illusion was difficult for me.

His head rocked. "And you heal vampires when you're drained."

When we broke from the forest, the gaggle of deputies had left, presumably with the corpse, and Chris waited, leaning against his game warden's truck. He straightened as he realized we were carrying Olivia, then hopped into his truck and drove toward us across the field beside the house. Phistrel and Leah set down the Dur-Alf stretcher.

I dropped to the grass, thirsty and tired. Part of me worried that the werewolf would chase us out here and finish us, and Dagen paced, eyes on the woods, with Aili chattering. I dug out my phone, checking the text messages from Finn. Marie had agreed, but I'd heard no word of their flight, or whether Finn would join them. His husband wouldn't be pleased if he did.

Leah sat beside me as Chris backed up to Olivia. "Any word?" she asked me.

"Not since she agreed. I expected them to have taken off by now."

Phistrel and Chris worked to get Olivia in the back of the truck. I wondered if we could get a ride across the fields to our vehicles.

"Want me to drive?" asked Leah.

I fished the keys out of my pocket. "You can carry me to the car if you want."

She chuckled, but she probably could. Our phones chirped, and I pulled mine up, expecting a message from Finn.

Neddie had sent us an email labeled "Russell Howard," with attachments. My split screen protector wouldn't let me open the files.

With a tilt of her phone, Leah showed me a picture of a serious, balding man with a bland background that screamed passport. Gray hair sprouted at the sides of his head, but the thick-rimmed glasses hid most of it. "Russell Howard."

I'd guessed as much.

She opened a document and began reading, "His aunt, Felicia Howard, has no ties to the arcane, but inherited the property eight years ago. There's a list of family members over the past few generations — actually since they first acquired the land. Only a few were considered involved with the arcane, and several of the older ones with question marks. To be expected."

"Why?"

"Lousy records back then. Oh."

I leaned forward, peering at her face and waiting for her to explain. "What?"

"Sorry. In 1954, a forty-eight-year-old arcane user, Elsie Dell, maiden name Elsie Howard, transitioned with the help of a Biera out of Canada. The Consociation registry has her returning to the homestead in 1969, but they lost her in 1982."

"Lost her?" I asked.

"The Consociation no longer had any reports on her whereabouts. They keep an aggressive tally of werewolves, vampires, and non-humans. Even if they are much more polite about it these days."

"David hinted at something similar. What do you suppose happened? That was thirty-five years ago."

"Thirty-six. Maybe the family didn't announce her death. We can't know the dynamics without having a discussion with Felicia, who was her younger sister. The middle sister, Margaret, Russell's mother, died in 1979."

Phistrel, studying his own phone, walked toward us. Dagen sat in the back of Chris's truck while Everek and Aili walked across the field. I pushed up to stand, not wanting to miss a ride.

Leah rose. "Elsie would have known Howard. I wonder if he tried to transition without a Biera. It requires more than just summoning Ya Keya."

I frowned. "I was always warned that all it took was contact."

"Rare," she said.

"What do you think?" asked Phistrel, turning to join us on the walk to the truck. "Any relevance?"

"Shows a potential interest. Neddie ever get anywhere with the local Biera?"

Phistrel pointed his cell at Dagen. "Dagen spoke with one of them last night. Closest is out of Whitefish. She never mentioned anything." He lowered his voice. "She would have if her theory was right."

Chris stood by his driver's door, watching us. "Room for two up front. Headed back to the house?" he asked.

Dagen stared at the woods, as if hungry to continue the hunt.

Phistrel climbed into the rear. "Yes. I'll drive the car back. We'll want to be there for Mika."

As I led the way to the passenger door, I whispered to Leah, "Everek won't bring Aili there, will he?"

"Gods, I hope not."

As Chris started the car, he studied us. "Looks like Olivia took the worst of it."

Leah, sitting in the middle, waved the broken strap of her purse at him. "Hardly. Besides, he wanted Kristen."

I tilted my head. "What?"

"He cleared us, but he kept checking on your approach. You saw how he ran for you once he had a chance."

We started across the bumpy field at a slow pace, and I replayed the attack. He hadn't waited for me to join the group before he pounced, but he also hadn't gone after Phistrel, the only other witch. That last dash of his *had* seemed focused. Dagen and Leah would have been up in a second. I shivered.

Everek had already left with Aili when we arrived at our vehicles. Dagen remained in the truck when Phistrel jumped out. Six other pickups were parked along the side of the roads with their gun racks empty. The hunters were in the area, despite Chris's attempts to divert them.

I circled the rear of the truck. "What did the Biera say?" I asked Dagen.

"Doesn't mean anything," she responded. Since the attack, she'd been curt, lacking any of her usual snark.

So, no new werewolf. "See you back at the house."

Dagen just huffed, glaring at the distant woods. From the bed of the truck, Olivia watched me, still drinking pouches; the swelling in her face had eased.

Leah moved the driver's seat back a little and adjusted the mirrors before we followed Phistrel.

"I'm thirsty." I pulled Mika's gun from my waistband and tucked it inside the glove box.

"Not hungry?" she asked with a smirk.

I flushed, usually the one to press for meals. "Not much. I do have to pee."

"Yeah, me too. Let them know we're going to stop."

As I texted on a group chat, Finn called me. I put it on speaker.

"Pyre and David are in the air. They'll be there in four hours. You don't need to pick them up. She got local FBI to leave a car. How you doing?"

"Tired. Is Neddie keeping you up to speed? Did you see the report on Russell Howard and Elsie?"

"You think Elsie is your bigfoot?" asked Finn.

"No," answered Leah, "Kristen is right about the facial structure. Primate, not canine. I got a clear view. Besides, she'd be over a hundred and bigfoot goes toe-to-toe with the werewolf, who's stronger than me or Dagen."

"How about the scent?" asked Finn.

Leah frowned, tightening her grip on the wheel. "Yeah, that is confusing. She smells close to a werewolf."

"What are we dealing with?" I asked them.

"I'd think the researchers would have plenty of ideas," Finn said.

I rolled my eyes. "Aili had plenty of questions."

"Aili? The author of *Akkadian to Napoleonic Werewolves*?"

"The same," said Leah drolly. "She tried to argue that I hadn't seen the facial structure correctly, and chastised that I hadn't gotten any photographs."

Finn laughed. "Hey, I studied the sigils in Howard's sanctum. I agree that he's messing with Tarus. Still no sign of him? He might have an answer about your demon."

I didn't like the demon being dubbed "mine," but only Phistrel had fully agreed about the presence. "We predict his body will be found near the burned mine. Haven't really had the time to follow that up. You think he summoned a demon?"

"The sigils lead toward that, but some are combined, which could have scary results." Finn sighed. "All right. Duty calls. The Consociation requests about Kristen's bigfoot are coming in left and right." I could hear the smile in his voice. "Be careful."

Leah chose the gas station on the curve by the lake instead of my usual spot, and we ended up with a couple of bags to bring back to the house. I downed a bottled latte before we returned to the road. Midmorning, the traffic had picked up, and at least one truck belonged to hunters. A pair of them shredded in the forest would likely be our next call.

The yard of the house seemed busy with the warden's truck and Mika's SUV parked out front. I had expected Everek to bring Olivia here.

"No Everek," I noted. "I owe him." With a stifled yawn, I unbuckled my seat belt. Under the bright sun, the residence appeared less gloomy as I stepped out. The fresh air held pine and wet soil.

"We could all use a rest. Mika should be back soon enough, if she isn't here already." Leah scooped up her broken purse with a disapproving frown. "I'm going to have to change."

I stretched. "Pop the trunk, would you? My purse is back there." The latch clicked in the back. Three ravens called from the trees beside the house, and a semi rumbled down the main highway, hidden by a thin copse. "It's getting warmer. Sixties, you think?" I asked as I dug into the back seat for our bags. A bottle of iced tea had escaped, and I leaned in to drag it from the floorboards.

Leah hadn't answered, so I glanced over the headrest to where she stood in the open driver's door. She dropped her purse. Her nails were growing long and black.

"He's here," she said.

TWENTY-SIX

My skin crawled, and I dropped the iced tea. "Where?" I whispered to Leah.

When I jerked out of the Subaru, I slapped the back of my head on the inside. My heart pounded in my throat, thudding when I pulled a shield from Dur-Alf. The effort drained me.

Gray spots dotted my vision as I peered first at the quiet house, then scanned to both sides. I didn't feel the demon's amplified terror yet; the rising apprehension was all me.

Leah's face had begun to transmogrify with her jaw jutting forward and fine hairs covering her skin. Her nostrils flared as her head dipped and turned in slight moves. I focused on her as my only warning for which direction the werewolf might attack us from. Blonde hair shifted as her ear twitched.

I remained frozen, a plump rabbit under a circling hawk.

A motion at the house pulled my eyes there.

Dagen crept out the front door, crouching and nails

extended. Chris followed with his weapon drawn. I exhaled in relief.

We had barely survived as a group; Leah and I wouldn't stand a chance alone. A dozen yards away, Dagen and Chris stalked in our direction, scanning to the sides, covering each other's backs. They saw us, but stayed silent.

Phistrel exited, flinging a Haven detection spell into the nearest trees to his right, then he stumbled as he pulled from Dur-Alf.

The three of them glowed white, along with a low shape hiding in the brush where Phistrel had sent his spell. He called out before I could, drawing the attention of Chris and Dagen to the werewolf.

Leah burst toward them with a growl.

A hand touched my back, and I jumped into the corner of the door with my shoulder.

"Easy," Mika said. Mer rippled over me, and my hands disappeared. "Back to the house. Follow the plan." They grabbed my hand. "Run. Eyes focused on the front door. Don't watch your feet."

I shook from being startled, but moved to comply, knocking my left knee painfully against the door.

Mika tugged with a firm but gentle grip, leading me wide around the bumper of the Subaru.

The werewolf, a blur trailing ghostly white, targeted Phistrel as Chris fired. Dagen and Leah both darted to intercept.

I faltered on my first step, but picked up speed. Mika led me toward the open front door, a few steps behind Phistrel. It felt cowardly, but I was the bait. With an air of desperation, I held onto the Dur-Alf shield in case I needed it.

Chris fired a second time, shifting smoothly with the werewolf in his sights. If his bullets hit, they had no effect.

Phistrel attempted a binding, then took a stride backward. As the werewolf darted to the side, the spell missed and dissipated.

At a full run, Dagen slammed into the werewolf, just ten feet from Phistrel. They went down in a snarl, rolling closer to the house.

My feet and arms turned a ghostly white under the Haven spell; Mika's shape formed, pulling me forward.

Dagen flew from the tangle, smashing into the building and buckling the siding. My heart skipped at the sight, then my throat tightened. Panic crawled up my sides. I flicked glances to the roof and the sides of the house, searching and dreading that I'd find the demon.

"C'mon." Mika tugged my hand.

My knees wobbled, but I kept running.

As Phistrel backed toward the front door, Leah collided with the werewolf. They spun on impact, and she flew aside in a spray of blood, toppling in the tall weeds.

We'd never make the door and the traps beyond. My teeth ached from clenching them.

Chris ran straight for Phistrel, who had nearly reached the front entrance.

The werewolf turned from where it had thrown Leah, ignoring her and Dagen. As it focused on Chris, then Phistrel, its eyes glinted red from the sun rising in the east. My blood ran cold.

I tripped, losing Mika's grip, and skidded into the dry grass that scraped my cheek raw. They cursed and darted back with exceptional nimbleness, grabbing my armpit.

"It's in the werewolf," I cried, pushing up to my knees. "The demon."

"Impossible."

I lurched forward as Mika's invisibility cloaked us, but the werewolf demon had seen me. "It is."

He grimaced as we disappeared, lunging for Chris, the closest of the witches.

With a flick, I tossed the spell I'd been holding. The shield formed perfectly in place, guarding Chris's left side.

The werewolf's roar echoed off the building as he crumpled against the unseen spell. Blood smeared on the shield, so perhaps one of Chris's bullets had hit, or Leah or Dagen had drawn blood.

Dagen crawled from beside the house, dragging her damaged leg. Leah had regained her feet, but blood soaked into her sleeve from the arm she held to her stomach.

Mika and I would never make the entry. Phistrel hung at the opening, pulling a binding spell from Dur-Alf. Chris spun into place beside him, but the werewolf recovered too quickly.

The demon werewolf sprang on all fours, clearing half the distance to them in one leap. He darted to the side, avoiding Phistrel's binding spell and Chris's bullet, then jumped.

I sagged as I pulled a shield from Dur-Alf as we ran, but I was too late.

With a swing mid jump, our attacker ripped into Phistrel's throat. Blood sprayed onto the house, pink with the overlay of Haven. Phistrel's body toppled to the entry with the force of the attack, rolling listlessly face down.

A raging shriek from Mika brought us to a halt. Mer rolled off us, exposing us.

Chris's gun fired, and the sharp crack seemed to slow time.

I registered the artificial terror inside, and couldn't stop shaking. My eyes were focused on Phistrel's body and the pool about his head and torso. Mika knelt beside me, digging at their ankle.

We'd stopped six feet away. The werewolf had leaped

farther than that in a single bound. I would die here, eaten by this horror. My mind couldn't process a plan of escape or attack.

The demon werewolf turned to us with gleeful eyes, even as it raked its claws into Chris.

The warden tried to spin away in time to save himself from a similar blow as Phistrel received, but his vest and shirt shredded on his shoulder as sharp nails tore into him and tossed him beside the house.

As I cast a futile shield between us and the werewolf, Mika fired a small backup into the spell, then cried a shrill curse.

When I reached into Dur-Alf, the bright sunshine surrounding us dimmed, and I couldn't manifest the energy to pull from it. Too weary to feel fear, I dropped to my knees but tried again.

Mika shifted to the side, avoiding my shield, and shot into the werewolf. He jumped to the side, not to avoid the bullet, but my shield.

Too smart, I thought.

The bullet hit his arm, and he recoiled. If Mika had used our special ammunition, it would poison him.

He bellowed with rage and slapped the gun, drawing blood and flesh from Mika's arm. Then, eyes on mine, he struck Mika with a backhand that brought the sound of breaking bone.

Leah called out, running toward us, but too far away.

I knelt, alone and helpless, digging for some spark of energy.

He knew my sorry condition and leaned down with hot, rancid breath, relishing in my perilous state.

A flash of blue reflected in his eye.

TWENTY-SEVEN

As bigfoot leaped toward us, I turned and drew my arms over my head.

Blood matted her shaggy side, and her attack proved ungainly, but she threw herself at him. She cried in a guttural croak, "Out!"

The demon werewolf swung before she impacted, but with little effect. I could smell their fur and blood; both were wounded.

My shield, still standing, withstood their weight as they crashed into it, grunting and snarling. I kicked a heel into the grass in an attempt to roll clear, but I just fell to my side.

They landed on my hip and feet, twisting my ankles and knees under their combined mass. I stifled a cry of pain, turning in a feeble plan to crawl away on my stomach, if I could get out from under them.

The realms of Tarus and Ya Keya wisped about them, possibly confirming that a demon possessed the werewolf, or that she came from Tarus. Both thoughts added to my fear. As they writhed and ripped at each other in a frenzy of dark wet fur, one of their claws scored my left thigh through my jeans. The tip of the nail snagged in my skin, and stuck, before it tore free.

I managed a wimpish roll, sliding my hip out from under them, but they spun, putting their full weight on my knees.

My fingers dug at the grass, and I brushed against Mika. The blue of Mer blended with the white of Haven over a motionless Mika, whose face pressed in the dirt and grass. I hoped they lived as I searched for the gun in desperate optimism.

Pain shot up my leg as the battling pair rose, one stepping their heavy weight on my ankle.

"Out!" shouted bigfoot again, her voice an angry roar.

As they danced away, grappling, kicking, and biting, their blood sprinkled on my outstretched arms. I pulled myself forward and pushed with my good ankle, driving my head and shoulders onto Mika's.

I couldn't run and had no energy to pull from the realms; the demon's terror hung limp against my exhaustion. With a turn of my head, I could only watch and hope that bigfoot might win.

She leaned into the werewolf more than attacked as blood ran wet down her neck and shoulders. When he ripped at her back in their clenching hold, black nails rendered red tears before her long fur matted against it.

He's going to win. Even as the thought crossed my mind, he kicked her away and out of my sight. *I'm next.*

Leah screamed as she leaped onto his back. Her bright shirt had opened at the seams of her shoulders and under her arms. She'd shifted so far into the werewolf form that her blonde hair had darkened, and tufts of fur sprouted from pointed ears. I recognized her only by her clothes.

"Phistrel," Mika murmured.

Surprised, and pleased that they lived, I twisted my head to find Mika gazing at me, unfocused. "Mika." I couldn't offer them hope. We were all doomed.

Mika's fingers grasped at Mer, turning it into turquoise light, then their eyes focused on mine. "Phistrel."

When Mika withdrew into Mer, my world vibrated at a higher pitch, as if I might be drawn into the other realm with her. The sounds of Leah and the werewolf snarling dulled and slowed, dropping to deep bass tones in my ears.

Through the pain and fear, I marveled at the experience.

The Merfolk forbade entry into their realm, and thus, little lore existed, and nothing like what I experienced. Peace pressed against the panic that the demon had bestowed upon me.

Time warped as I sank to the grass where I'd leaned on Mika's body. Stalks of green waved slowly. A moment of calm bubbled around me as the rich scents of growth and life rose from the moist ground. My skin tingled with a languid crawl up my arms and neck.

In a snap, all sound returned. A painful cry erupted from Leah before her body soared over mine, rolling in the grass.

Inexplicably, some of my energy had recovered from the interaction with Mer. However, I had not time to consider as the panic returned. Still, I rolled, readying to grasp into Dur-Alf.

Agony spiked through my knees and ankle, leaving me twisted on the ground with my shoulders flat and hip unyielding.

The werewolf staggered to me, obviously wounded from the battle, but still the best for wear. A trio of red slashes cut from under his left eye to his upper lip. Despite the damage and sluggishness of his body, his eyes shone as he reached down for me.

I sucked in foul air as claws pierced my upper arms and he lifted me into the air. My head tilted back, and my legs dangled, their pain forgotten.

The melded twilight and midnight of Ya Keya and Tarus whirled about the demon werewolf. With a shake of his unnaturally strong arms, my head snapped forward, and he grinned with bloody teeth.

My muscles screamed as I moved my hands, pulling at Tarus. Like a vampire, a demon could not return from their realm of their own volition.

I pulled the pitch black of Tarus over us.

My captor howled in rage, throwing me away from him. I hit soft dust, pain radiating from all my twisted limbs and shredded skin.

As in my previous travel to Tarus, unseen creatures scrabbled about with nails on rock or feet scuffing dust. Unlike before, they were running away, not toward me.

A dull, red glow, like embers under ash, emanated from the figure in front of me. A man, balding with white sprouts of hair behind his ears, stood shaking with tremors while his pale skin roiled with an underglow of red.

Russell Howard. He appeared the right age, though his face bulged and distorted as if something inside fought to escape. His eyes flashed piercing red, illuminating the desolate landscape around us.

The demon, it's escaping. My fingers dug into dust, searching for the Earth realm.

The demon's imposed terror had left me, but I imagined it possessing me once it discarded Russell. The fire in his eyes brightened to an intensity that made me wince and squint, though it remained red.

I turned my head aside as my fingers dug into a slick

realm, not the thick mud of Earth. Rich purple gelled about my hand, and I shook it free. Different realms would touch Tarus, along with Earth, Haven, and Ya Keya. I shivered at what might lie beyond.

Light exploded from Russell, eliciting shrieks from the escaping creatures. It dimmed in a flash, leaving my sight dim under a red glow.

When Russell fell to his knees before me, I jerked, causing my legs to twitch in pain. "They lied," he croaked. "The Red Aegis is a lie."

His skin sagged over an emaciated form that showed bones where the wrinkled flesh did not fold over itself. The man's eyes were dead black pits. The corpse slapped to the dust, raising a cloud.

The demon glowed, an amorphous red cloud whirling and writhing in the air ten feet above me. Features of eyes, teeth, and horns threatened to form from the mass, but it seemed out of control.

Then, three bright glowing eyes rotated to create a triangle. More flickered at the edges, as if trying to join. They were looking at me.

I closed my eyelids tight and reached for Earth. The muddy sensation at my fingertips, I pulled the realm about me.

TWENTY-EIGHT

I drew in a lungful of fresh air as I opened my eyes to a bright blue sky. "Earth," I whispered.

The sun shone from behind me, but high enough to cause me to squint. My breath caught, remembering Phistrel's death. The others would need help.

Because of the sharp aches, I couldn't move my limbs, at least not until a throaty voice asked, "Russell?"

Pain racked my body, but I rolled to my side, one elbow managing to prop myself up. Bigfoot sat cross-legged, an arm's reach from me. I would have shuffled away if my arms didn't feel like they would slough off at the shoulders.

My interaction with Mer had left me enough energy that I could have reached for a binding spell, but she had fought with us, not against us. "Russell?" How did she know his name?

It didn't seem that any part of her fur hadn't been soaked with blood. "My nephew," she said with slow deliberation, as if it were difficult.

I frowned. "You are Elsie?"

She nodded once. "Russell?"

"Oh, I'm so sorry. He died when the demon left him." I swallowed, recognizing my part in her nephew's death. In her condition, I'm not sure what she could or would do in revenge.

Elsie closed her eyes with a weary sigh. "Promised to look after." She didn't appear to blame me, and it wasn't really my fault; Russell had become possessed.

I mixed Earth and Haven on myself, enough to allow my arms and legs to move. Everything, especially my ankle, could use a ton more. The strange experience with Mer had revitalized me, but not to full strength, and others would need help. With a slight gasp, I shifted to sit up, hands on my knees.

Dagen had collapsed near Chris, but both their chests rose, as did Leah's a few feet away from me. Phistrel's corpse lay at the door.

"Are you going to survive?" It seemed rude to ask what Elsie was now. She had been a werewolf.

When she didn't open her eyes or reply, I continued. "Can I try to heal you?"

Elsie didn't move, so I blended Earth and Haven, reached out with one hand, and let it flow over her.

Her eyes shot open. "You can't." Then, as I stopped, her head tilted, and she raised an arm, flexing her clawed hand. "You can." Awe tinged her voice.

I offered a sheepish smile and continued. The sensations that splashed back from her were of a deep sorrow — and far more pain than I felt.

"Kristen?" asked Leah from behind. Her muted tone held inquiry and threat.

"We're good. Leah, meet Elsie, Russell Howard's aunt." I didn't turn, focusing my smile on Elsie. "Elsie, this is my partner and friend, Leah. She's a werewolf."

Elsie watched Leah. "I know."

The ground scuffed behind me, and the sound of a hand brushing off clothes followed. Leah cleared her throat, limping toward us. "Aunt Elsie? Last I heard, you were a werewolf."

With a rocking that might have been amusement, Elsie breathed a sigh. "I've broken a cardinal rule of my kind. An oath, if you will. What's done is done." She spoke at a measured pace, pausing at points. "I am what you would become if you stepped into Ya Keya."

Leah stopped beside me. "There is lore."

"Most of it, correct."

"You can't return to the Earth realm from Ya Keya." Leah's statement held a question, since obviously Elsie sat with me.

"Part of the incorrect lore. Also, part of the oath I took."

With a roll of my aching shoulders, I stopped the healing, sensing I'd brought Elsie to a better state. I needed to help the others. My chest hollowed, considering Phistrel.

"You can use magic," I surmised.

She looked aside, eyebrows rising in a human expression. "Not as a witch, Merfolk, or dwarf might. Let's say it is limited." Elsie raised her hand in frustration. "Oath."

I nodded, not wanting to push. "You were trying to save your nephew. Do I have it right?"

Her face turned sad. "I promised his mother. When he summoned the demon, I felt it. He was always too ambitious and arrogant." She gestured to the surrounding area. "This is my hunting grounds. I can sense things from Ya Keya. The demon took Russell, and then it bonded with Ya Keya to take the form of power."

Leah scoffed. "What were you going to do?"

Elsie cocked her head up. "Exorcise it. We have that ritual at the house. The demon did not burn that."

"Russell mentioned something called the Red Aegis," I said. "What is that?"

She shrugged. "I've never heard the term. Perhaps a ritual?"

No, it was someone who lied to him. I didn't mention it. "What will you do now? Return?" I raised my fingers and snapped them, wincing.

"Thanks to your healing, yes. I had thought I might die here and leave a mystery." She grunted. "I don't suppose we could keep this out of the Consociation's grasp?" Elsie cocked her head. "Oath."

Leah spun, searching behind us.

Two hunters in camo and orange vests were running from the woods to the south. They had spotted Elsie, or at least something dark and furry from that distance.

"Thank you," Elsie said, "for freeing Russell." She raised her hand and snapped her fingers, disappearing with a blue flash.

With an obvious limp, Leah stalked toward the hunters. "Out of here. FBI business." In her ragged clothes, she didn't command their immediate compliance.

Chris, however, stood shakily, and added his voice. "Turn around. You are on private property under the joint authority of the FWP and FBI." His uniform, while scuffed, dirty, and stained with blood, appeared somewhat official, from a distance.

The hunters stopped, considered their options, then retreated.

I focused on Dagen. She had stirred at Chris yelling nearby, but hadn't risen. We had to check on her.

After a false start, I glared at my ankle. Twisted, I hoped. With what little energy I had left after healing Elsie, I preferred saving myself until I saw what I could do for Dagen. Chris and Leah were at least vertical.

"An assist?" I waved a hand at Leah. "My ankle isn't the best at the moment."

As she limped over, she bore a grim expression. "I would have liked more answers from Elsie. Mika back in Mer?"

"Yes." My report would take two days to describe everything, and Marie would want it all in detail. Keeping my bad leg straight, I shifted to my good foot and raised a hand to Leah.

Chris knelt by Dagen, studying her, then Phistrel's body. "I heard some of that conversation," he said as I hobbled toward him with Leah at my side. "I am not sure I was ready for all of this."

"So, a demon inside a werewolf," Leah said. "I guess that explains the strength. Possessed humans get pumped up."

We passed close to Phistrel's corpse. "Mika was pretty torn up about Phistrel," I said.

Leah glanced over. "Mika brought him on about twelve years ago."

"Baby of the team," murmured Dagen, raising her head. "I'm going to kill that sonofabitch."

"Too late, buttercup." Leah eased me down beside Dagen. "From what I hear, Kristen took him home."

"To Ya Keya?" Dagen's leg twisted wrong at the knee joint; she'd dragged herself ten yards trying to reach Russell.

"Tarus," I corrected. "We talked to Elsie, and she said that —"

"Who the hell is Elsie?"

"Bigfoot. Russell's aunt. That's a long story." I turned at distant sirens pealing in the midmorning quiet.

"How long was I out?" Dagen asked. "Where's Mika?" Her tone became harsh and demanding. "Is Mika okay?"

"Mer," I said in a calm tone. Mixing Earth and Haven, I started healing, surprised at the amount of pain, but not at the anger. "Turn over."

"I don't want to spill out." Dagen grumbled.

The sense of torn flesh in her abdomen came through the healing. "Damn, Dagen." I worried I wouldn't have enough energy to get her stable.

"Whatever, keep me occupied, doc. Explain how this Tarus is home for the asshole."

I settled to get comfortable as Chris stood to focus on the drive and the impending arrival of the local deputies. We could hope Buckley had sent Rebekah.

My words were slow and calm. "Russell called a demon, who possessed him, who then interacted with Ya Keya to become a werewolf."

"Transitioned," she corrected. "So why the hots for witches?"

"No clue." Multiple sirens pierced through the woods from the highway. "So, I ended up pulling Russell through to Tarus, the demon left, he died, and I came back here. That's when I found Elsie."

Leah watched the drive. "We had a lovely chat. Family stuff. Oh, and how she was a werewolf who moved to Ya Keya and figured out a way to come back and hunt her old stomping grounds."

"Impossible." Dagen's voice came out in a tight huff.

My energy sagged as we fought to reknit her body. "Someone should call Everek."

"Wimp," said Dagen.

Leah slipped out her phone and knelt beside me. "Don't go too far."

Tires sounded on dirt as vehicles turned into the drive. My vision shook slightly as I focused on Chris, standing behind my rental.

"Hey, sweetie," Leah said, "we could use some help, if you've got time."

The deputies slowed when they spotted Chris, then pulled up to each side of him.

"Sure, if Olivia's feeling better, bring her along." Leah scowled. "Wait, where are you?"

Buckley, glaring from the driver's side, didn't bother getting out, but his lackeys did. *No sign of Rebekah.* I'd have rather she'd come out.

"My room?" squeaked Leah. "I've barely used it. You better not have messed with my things in the bathroom. Oh, wait, have Olivia pick me out a shirt, the lavender one with the roses." She tugged at the split seams under her arms.

Chris faced three deputies who peered at us, and likely Phistrel's body.

The world tilted, and Leah smacked my shoulder. "Enough."

I let go of the spell, hoping I'd gotten a good start on Dagen.

"No, not you, Everek. Hoist up those suspenders and bust a move." She placed her phone beside me. "How are you two doing?"

"Fabulous," murmured Dagen.

"I'm fine," I said, trying to sound cheery.

"Liars."

TWENTY-NINE

I stood as Everek pulled past the deputies and Chris, still at a standoff on the drive. Leah had gone inside to get us water. I felt the idea of stepping over Phistrel's corpse uncomfortable, even rude.

"Everek's here," I told Dagen. She remained on her stomach, though I'd tried to convince her to show me the wound.

"Yay," she said in a sarcastic, bland tone.

He bounced the truck around the parked cars and curved to pull the truck up beside Dagen, blocking the view of the deputies. After he opened the door, he dropped his bag to the ground, then kicked out his cowboy boots and landed beside it. "Damn, someone got rough with the guard dog." His grin faded as he caught sight of Phistrel. The illusion frowned, turning to me.

I shook my head. "He didn't make it." The passenger side door of his truck creaked open, and I glimpsed Olivia.

"Mika?" he asked.

"Back to Mer."

Leah stepped out of the house with water before he

could ask about her. Everek dragged his bag to Dagen, still focused on Phistrel's body.

Olivia carried a pile of clothes as she walked around the hood of the truck. Her face held a few yellow bruises, but the worst of the swelling had reduced. She wore the same ragged attire. "What is the situation?" Her eyes flicked to Phistrel and Dagen. "In regard to the werewolf?"

"Tarus." I faltered, stepping toward her, since my legs didn't want to join me. While Leah brought water and took her clothes, I relayed Mika's retreat, my trip to Tarus, and the details about Elsie.

Leah changed her top, using the door to Everek's truck to hang clothes. "You know the Consociation is going to have a fit that we let Elsie go, right?"

I didn't, but grimaced as she knew their motives better than I did. "She needed to get someplace and heal."

"Put that in the report." Leah scoffed.

With a frown, I searched Olivia's expression. She didn't comment about Leah's warning. "There was an author, Antre, who detailed an elusive creature with bigfoot's description. There was theory much later, within the past two centuries, that werewolves trapped in Ya Keya might be the origin. However, I would not count on Elsie's recounting."

"Why not?" I asked.

Leah emerged with her fresh shirt, still appearing roughed up. "Because Olivia is the skeptic."

Olivia studied me. "I do believe your recital of the events."

"Thanks." I sipped my water.

Two more vehicles rumbled down the drive, and I stepped to the side, peering around Everek's truck. A jeep and pickup pulled behind my rental, bearing the game warden's insignia. Chris stood alone as the deputies returned to their cars.

"Where's Aili?" I asked, grateful that the dwarf hadn't accompanied Everek.

He had the brown muddy flow of Earth pulled up and worked it against an angry tangle of healing flesh across Dagen's stomach. "In the bar, waiting for me. She's got a posse of seven researchers, Merfolk and Dwarves, gathered, with two more landing tonight."

"The bar?" I asked.

Leah sniffed. "The lodge has a couple of tables." She sighed. "I'll be sneaking up to my room tonight if we spend the night."

Dagen rolled her head back. "I'll be good to travel."

"You won't," corrected Everek.

Olivia gestured to the house. "We need you to unravel the wards, Kristen. We can ask Chris, as well."

I finished my bottle and headed for Phistrel's body. At his neck, his torn flesh had darkened, blending into the drying blood. His face pressed against the grass, so I couldn't see much of the damage. My interaction with him had been limited, but I still felt his loss. We all took this risk.

Before I entered, I texted Jade.

Worst is over. I've got some reports, then I'll be heading to spend tomorrow with you. I love you, honey.

She didn't reply immediately, and I stuffed my phone back in my pocket. At least she could stop worrying about me.

Phistrel had set the wards for easy disassembly. We hadn't been up against a witch, just an arcane user who called a demon. I moved through them at a steady pace, first the entry, then the back door and windows. The air in the house hinted at breakfast and coffee.

While I worked in a bedroom, muffled voices sounded at the entry. I'd never had to deal with a member of the Consociation dying, so I didn't know if Phistrel would be released to the local coroner or not. I somehow doubted it.

Olivia appeared in the doorway and offered another bottle of water. "How did the demon know how to connect with Tarus?" she asked. "A lich might have the knowledge, but a demon?"

I opened my water. "A question for Tomas or Marie. I know so little about demons." One of the many things I'd dig into when I got back to Atlanta.

Boots sounded across the floor, growing closer, so Olivia turned. Chris appeared in the hall. He'd been bruised about the jaw, and a fresh bandage covered his right hand and wrist.

"Dagen said you took care of it?" he asked.

"The problem is trapped in Tarus."

"She didn't have a lot of details." He fished for information, and I stalled by taking another sip.

Her head turning to him on a swivel like an owl, Olivia responded. "The Consociation will have concerns that we involved you as much as we did. Mika can justify a certain amount of exposure based on exigent circumstances, but that has ended. They might be willing to release details, but we can't."

Chris tilted his head with acceptance. "Fair. I've got the scene secured with FWP, but they've got questions I won't answer. Reporters are nipping at the outer edges."

"Buckley?" I asked with a smirk.

"That lovely man is filing a complaint, but two of his deputies are stationed at the road, supposedly keeping the reporters back. I think they're keeping an eye on our activities." Chris offered a smile toward the end of his explanation.

I like him. Along with Phistrel, and likely the others, he'd get his own character card. *Knight Errant, perhaps.*

He took a deep breath, shifted to leave, and asked, "Anything I can get you?"

Leah called from the main room. "Lunch. Kristen wants lunch."

I blushed.

Chris chuckled as he left us. "I hope everyone likes burgers."

"Cheese," Leah whispered loud enough for me to hear. "I like mine rare."

Olivia followed me to the next room, and Leah joined us while I tugged apart the ward.

"I called Finn. Updated him. He got a message to Pyre. She'll call us when she lands."

From the main room came a shrill Merfolk curse, and I knew Mika had returned. For them, it might have only been a minute. Fingers in the middle of plucking a thread of Dur-Alf, I hurried to finish while Leah and Olivia scurried out.

Mika's pained cries nearly had me in tears. As the voices intensified, I worked slower. Their team needed time to mourn.

I considered Marie, knowing she would never publicly put on a display if I died. *Finn would.* As I finished, I peered out the window as the clouds drifted fleeting shadows on the grass and trees outside. We'd succeeded, at a cost.

When I went into the main room, Leah was holding Mika at the entry where Everek worked on Phistrel's body. Olivia turned from watching them. I stood apart, hovering near the dining table with my empty bottle.

Mika pulled back from Leah, noticing me, then ambled

toward me. The spectacles had disappeared, and their eyes were red and wet.

"Thank you," Mika said, pulling me into a hug.

I didn't question, just held them until they cried in silence on my shoulder. As expected, I couldn't hold my own tears back. We hugged for longer than I usually endured, then parted.

"I've the overview from Leah. I'll need the details." Mika wiped their face. "Once Everek has Phistrel and Dagen ready for transport, we'll find someplace quiet to have lunch."

"Chris is bringing burgers."

Mika nodded wearily and gestured to the dining table. "This is quiet."

A couple hours later, the clouds had cleared the sky again, I'd answered Mika's every question, and the burgers and fries were gone; mine at least. Finn had coordinated local FBI to replace Chris and his wardens, mainly to keep out reporters and hunters.

Tired, I slouched in the chair beside Leah. Olivia sat straight-backed next to Mika on the other side of the table.

"One last thing," I said to Mika, though I would have liked to keep the topic private. "When you entered Mer, I received a spike of energy. Is that known?"

Mika flashed a nod. "The connection between Mer and Earth has always had more — friction than others. We've studied the vibrational differences in detail for many centuries. I can suggest some research if you'd like. There are plenty of references to the phenomenon you describe."

"Sure. Thank you." I'd be as likely to get to those as the database Tomas had built.

Leah's and my phone dinged with messages. She spoke before she pulled hers out. "Pyre's here."

Sure enough, a set of coordinates followed her simple

request for a report. Mika pulled out their phone and started typing.

Leah rose, and I followed a little slower.

"We'll be joining you," said Mika. Their usual affable nature had dulled, understandably.

With a flick at my sleeve, Leah reminded me that I'd want to change out of my bloody sweatshirt. I'd healed the holes closed, but would need to finish when I built up some energy. For now, a fresh change would be in order.

CHAPTER

THIRTY

I pulled into the parking lot of Brannigan's pub, already growing busy in the midafternoon, though it was Saturday.

"Mika." David walked onto the asphalt, dressed impeccably in a dark suit. His tone did not hint at any teasing or even joviality, so I knew he'd heard about Phistrel. The last time I'd seen him meet with Mika had been very different.

As they hugged, Leah tugged at my sleeve, heading around me for the entrance. Olivia remained with us. The lively bar smelled of good food that made me wish I'd held back on lunch. A fair number of people grouped around tables, talking and laughing, which jostled my somber mood.

Marie sat alone at a table for six, sipping on a beer. She gave us a nod, then waved at a server.

"Fly out here for the beer?" asked Leah.

"It seems so." Marie studied us as if gauging our bruises and injuries as we took seats across from her. "Olivia, you've looked better."

"I have," agreed Olivia, taking a seat near the window.

A young, pleasant girl let me order whatever local beer Marie worked on. Olivia ordered iced tea, despite the server's suggested options. Leah took her time with light flirting until Mika could join us and order a Manhattan.

Marie reached across the table and patted Mika's hand. "I'm sorry about Phistrel. It's not easy, losing one."

"Thank you, Pyre. Last time, it was me with consolations for you." Mika's voice cracked. "Sorry to bring you all the way out here."

"I'll make use of it." Marie nodded to me. "I've gotten preliminaries. Hit me with the high notes. I'll wait for the report to get the details."

While I retold events around the occasional interruptions by the server, I nursed my beer. Marie listened without question until I mentioned Russell Howard dying in Tarus.

"What were his exact words?" she asked.

"Um, 'they lied, the Red Aegis is a lie,' nothing more; he barely got that out."

Her expression tightened. Even David, sniffing at some house wine, raised his eyebrows.

Mika cocked their head. "Pyre, what is it?"

"Can't. I want a look at the mine and Russell Howard's house." Her intense tone silenced the table.

"Yeah, sure." Mika waved their empty glass at the passing server.

I continued describing Elsie's relationship, but Marie appeared absorbed in her own thoughts. Leah jumped in during my conversation with bigfoot, and Olivia offered questions as to the veracity of Elsie's statements, but I kept wondering about Marie's interest in the Red Aegis. It rose to the first thing I'd look up in the database. However, Mika hadn't understood the importance of the term.

David raised his glass. "To disappointing your family."

"I had a punderful father figure." I blushed, putting down my beer. Only my second, but I'd be driving.

"Speaking of disappointing, how did camping go?" asked David. He winced when Leah kicked him.

Marie tapped on the table and spoke absently. "Take a couple extra days, Kristen. If you can work it out with your daughter."

With one finger, I rubbed at the beads of sweat on the glass. "You mean reschedule my flight? I can do that."

Marie just nodded.

THIRTY-ONE

In a lazy current, I floated in a tube under the shade on a Sunday afternoon. My lotion smelled like coconut, making me think of warmer beaches. I'd soon be returning to the Atlanta heat, so I enjoyed the cooler weather.

"Mom?" Jade held us together with her hand pressed into the black rubber. Her own tube had a red line around the top.

I rolled my head back and to the side. "Yes, honey?"

Jade moved her hand to my arm, pulling up the short sleeve of the T-shirt to expose the bruises on my shoulder. Yellow, dime-sized marks were left from the werewolf's claws. "Do you have to do this? Your job?"

My first thought went to Phistrel; I hadn't told Jade about him, or much concerning the case. Then I remembered the other bodies and nodded. "It helps people."

She turned to watch the sun-sparkled water. "I don't want to lose you."

After how close I'd come, I couldn't promise her it

would never happen. "I know, and I try to be careful — all the time."

Meghan laughed from the shore, drawing Jade's attention. My daughter's hand drifted off my arm.

"Jade! Time for the hike. Sssnakesss!" Meghan splashed into the water.

With a kick, Jade pushed out of her tube in the shallow water, then turned to me with bright eyes. "You still coming?"

"Of course, honey." I pulled down my wet T-shirt and struggled to get up, capsizing to the girls' laughter.

I couldn't hide the bruises on my legs, but no one had commented on them, or my choice to put a T-shirt on over my bathing suit. Still, Cheryl's eyes flicked over my body before she forced a smile. "If you need rest, you know you don't have to go."

With a shrug, I smiled to disperse her concern. "I'm making every minute count."

"Nice of them to give you more time."

"It is." I headed to my car to grab hiking clothes.

Russell Howard had intrigued Marie, and she remained in Montana. I'd likely never know why. Mika had been clear that they and Olivia were returning to Arizona, since Phistrel had a wife there. Dagen had already returned.

I grabbed my phone and checked to see how many more work emails I'd received. The count had topped seventy as of this morning, all asking for reports on Elsie. I'd already started the report and planned on getting more done this evening.

Ten more had come in, but one had a different subject: "Re: Red Aegis." That caught my interest, as Marie had reacted to it. Some analyst of the Consociation, Zach Graves, wanted confirmation and clarification. I scratched my wet scalp. "Tonight," I murmured, and put the phone away. Extended vacation or not, Marie still expected her reports, as did everyone else.

After a quick change in the bathroom, I accepted the walking stick that Harry offered with some ceremony and piled into the rear seat of the Turner's truck with Jade and Meghan.

Jade squeezed my hand, obviously excited. "Half of the trail is up into the mountain. There's a waterfall, and we climb to the top."

"Good," I said. "I need a change of altitude."

AFTERWORD

Review here - https://www.amazon.com/review/create-review/?&asin=B0FH5L41ZX

A quick thanks and a hope that you enjoyed this story, if you did then a review is always helpful.

I've been working on my world's Bigfoot for a while, and hope to meet Elsie in the future.

Would you be interested in a free short from David's perspective? An incident in his past? You can download from BookFunnel a very quick read. It'll sign you up for a mailing list during the download, but it won't activate unless you confirm on the follow up email.

David's Journal #21 https://BookHip.com/FRQGMPM

GRIMOIRE APPENDIX

Demon

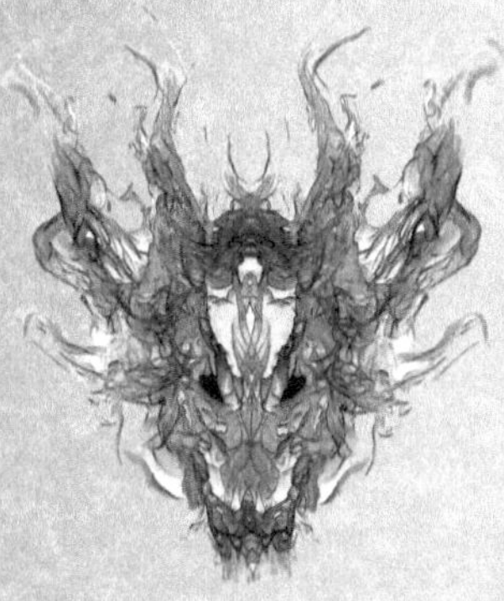

A demon is a rare inhabitant of the Tarus Realm who can be summoned to the Earth realm or cross of its own intent if given an opening. [1]

Their summoned forms often are a nightmarish mirror of their summoner with features designed to terrorize, such as claws, fangs, and horns. [1][2] Highly intelligent, they feed on strong emotions such as panic or rage. [2][3]

They are reported to rely on physical attributes for attack, but have been known to compel humans to act out their violence. [2][3]

(Cont. next page; Accounts of Demons in Tarus)

[1] Read Tinkanchtners's The Art of Demonic Summoning

[2] Read Kizurra's Referene on Tarus Cryptids Page 26 to 47

[2] Read Carey's Of Demons and Jinns

Dragon-shifter

 The portion of a dragon exposed in the Earth realm which can mimic the aspect of a human.
 Most of what is known about dragon-shifters has come from archaic grimoires with questionable translations. [1][2] There is at least one resident on Earth to coordinate with the Consociation. [3] Reportedly, a dragon-shifter is an exact replica of a human, unless they intend otherwise. [2][4] A witch would know on contact.
 The details of their craft ability are shrouded in myth due to their self-expulsion from the Earth realm prior to the Akkadian wars was preceded by a slow withdrawal during the prior era. [1][2][4] They openly apologize for their interference with man, resulting in the rituals that brought about the vampires and werewolves. [3][5]

(Cont. next page; Role in Consociation)

[1] Read Yin's Volume IV of Realm Studies Pages 1340 to 1489

[2] Read Wooley's Anecdotal Studies of Salmhalla

[3] Read Ferno's Presentation of the Consociation

[4] Read Inhai Du Anya's Scriptures of the High Dragons Page 1-72

[5] Read Sover's On Madness

Draugr / Draughr

A common inhabitant of Tarus who can be summoned to the Earth realm, or cross of its own intent if given an opening. Territorial they tend toward an unusual compunction to protect valuables.

Tall and strong they present as humanoid on Earth with no skin and sharp black nails. They possess reflexes and speed beyond humans.[1] Savage and instinctual on a physical level. Relatively low intelligence.

Magical or Arcane abilities: None

Note the Akkadian ritual listed in the 1911 appendix

[1]Read Maorin's Journal for an in-depth biological reference compilation of Merfolk research of the Draugr

Dwarf / Dwarves

Humanoid residents of Dur-Alf with a proclivity for exploration and research. Their earliest interactions with humans caused a wider disturbance than expected and their own sanctions for crossing to Earth were ignored by many of their more independant scholars and explorers. Brief conflicts existed between individuals as witches developed the ability to pass into the Dur-Alf realm.

Small in mass and stature, their biology is similar to Earth mammals. [1]

Conflicts erupted between humans and dwarves [2] as human witches and arcane users began to cross realms. Dwarves are especially biased against vampires.

(Cont. next page; Magical and Arcane usage)

[1] Read Maorin's Understanding Dwarven Physiology and Psyche

[2] Read Thant's War on Human Mutation

Kuru Kuru

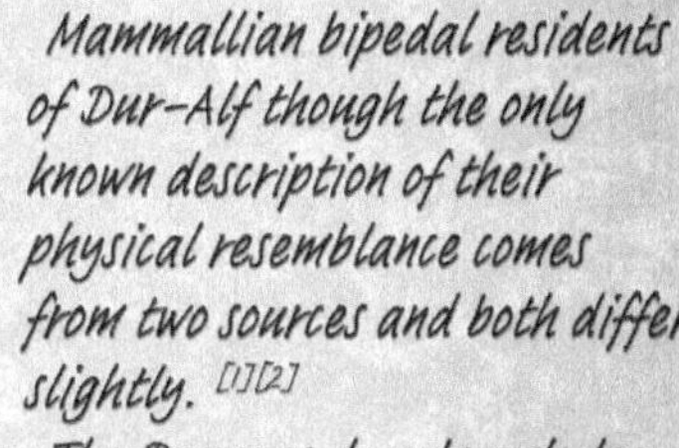

Mammallian bipedal residents of Dur-Alf though the only known description of their physical resemblance comes from two sources and both differ slightly. [1][2]

The Dwarves do acknowledge their presence and the Kuru Kuru have been given access to the Consociation. [3] They speak only to the Dragon delegation there and have some relationship with Dragons. [4]

Small in mass and stature, their biology is similar to Earth mammals with a flattened muzzle. Reports differ on fur (pictured), or with feathers. [1][2][3]

(Cont. next page; Magical suppositions)

[1] Read Kainin's Guide to Dur-Alf, Eden of the Realms

[2] Read Emily Randolp's Memoirs Among the Sprites

[3] Read Daesalu's Biography of Talat

[4] Read Ono Seyo's Conspiracy of the Consociation

Merfolk / Mer

Mer, called Merfolk by the Consociation, have the ability to transform into similar mammalian shapes upon interrealm movement. [1]

Little is known about their unaltered form except that it is a sea mammal of some type, hypothesized to be porpoise-like. [2]

Their longstanding habitation of Earth's oceans ceased at the point when Earth witches and arcane users began using the Mer realm in magic which coincided with the interrealm movement of humans to Dur-Alf. [3] Merfolk returned to Earth during the formation of the Consociation at the urging of the dwarves with whom they had long enjoyed diplomacy and trade. [4]

Many Mer research and work on Earth as part of their proposal to the Consociation for admittance. [5]

(Cont. next page; the impact of Merfolk on magical use by witches and the arcane)

[1] Read Sienna's Treatise on Earth's Devastation

[2] Read Tino Vangian Biography of Venis: Traitor of Mer

[3] Read Sienna's Treatise on Mer Isolation

[4] Read Tino Vangian Biography of Venis: Traitor of Mer

[5] Read Tino Vangian's Biograpy of Sienna

Revenant

An inhabitant of Tarus which can be summoned to the Earth realm, or cross of its own intent if given an opening.

Disembodied in the Earth realm, they will seek to possess a humanoid corpse, or living entities with a weakened consciousness such as comotose or those near death.

Their corporeal control depends greatly on their prior experience.[1]

They range in intelligence and will avoid confrontation where possible.

Expellation is relatively simple depending on the skill of the witch.[2] Vampires have an innate ability to remove Revenants from their possessed hosts.

Magical or Arcane abilities: None

[1]Read Rasputin's Walks Among the Undead for a detailed observance of summoned Revenants

[2]See Appendix from 1892 - reference Possession

Vampire

A vampire is a human-born crossover to the Tarus realm. They are infected with a Tarus symbiotic life form initially misunderstood as a form of magic inherited from Tarus. [1] The infection can be summoned, gained through prolonged contact with Tarus, or transferred by blood-to-blood transfer with a vampire. [2]

The human cells are mutated to a far more resilient state and can be controlled to an extent which allows the vampire to change facial features and extend their life. [1] [3] Strength and speed are are increased with minimal muscular and bone alterations. [4] Vampires are entirely resistant to infection, disease, and toxins. [3] Mental acuity does not change. Emotional reactions remain, though extended life spans have brought interesting results. [1] [3] [4] [5]

(Cont. next page; the Tarus symbiote)

[1] Read Tonsun's *Illuminating the Mystery*

[2] Read William Beckett's *Becoming a Legend*

[3] Read Annan's *Study on Mutation*

[4] Read Anonymous *Confessions of Self-Hatred*

[5] Read Macrin's *Sapien Emotive Reponses* Pages 21-88

Werewolf / Dreamer / Hunter

Born human they have developed a psychic and realm connection to Ya Keya. They are affected by their interactions and develop biological alterations. The connection can be summoned, by a ritual interaction with the bodily fluids of a mature werewolf, or through intense submersion in Ya Keya.[1] Longevity varies [2]

Transmuted form:
They gain 15–20% more mass directly from the Ya Keya realm. Reflexes, strength, and speed increase by 10–30% beyond their human norms. Eyesight and hearing are more acute though more age dependant than other attributes.[2]

(Cont. next page; loss of Magic and Arcane usage)

[1]Read Kizurra's History of Akkadian Werewolves - the Dawn

[2]Read Demot's Monograph for an in-depth biological reference

Dur-Alf

Visible indications are a dark-green color and a crumbling or dusty consistency.

Dur-Alf is a planet realm similar to Earth in that it orbits a singular star; it is the fourth of eight known bodies in the system and does not have any satellites. There are major land-locked bodies of water and large polar ice caps. [1] Rivers and lakes abound in most regions except near equatorial deserts. The seasons are mild, and wildlife is plentiful. [1] [2] The only known transplants from Earth are kestrels and a variety of water birds including swans, geese, ducks, and kingfishers. [1] [2] [3]

Humans are no longer welcome or tolerated in the Dur-Alf realm. [4]

Known bordering realms: Earth, Mer, Salmhalla, Mer, and Tique (described as a hostile realm [5]).

(Cont. next page; Known Species)

[1] Read Kainan's Guide to Dur-Alf; Eden of the Realms

[2] Read Emily Randalp's Memoirs Among the Sprites

[3] Read Yin's Volume VI of Realm Studies Pages 1289 to 1402

[4] Read Consociation Guidelines for Interrealm Treaties. Page 157.

[5] Read Yin's Volume VIII of Realm Studies Page 44 to 399

Haven

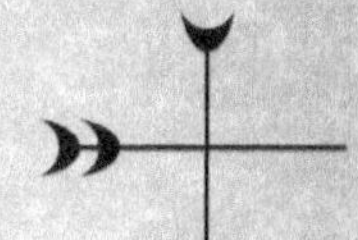

  Visible indication is a white mist of a thick consistency reminding some observers of cotton candy.
  Haven is a plane realm of breathable air, moisture in the form of clouds or mist, and no gravity. The ambient light is bright. No lifeforms or other identifying components have been found in the realm. [1][2][3]

  Dwarves and Merfolk have often used Earth merely to experience the realm. [3][4] Other than the magic available by touching the realm, little of use exists there.
  Hypothesises exist as to alternates states. [3][5][6]
  Known bordering realms: Earth, Salmhalla, and Tarus.
  (Cont. next page; Consociation Prohibitions)

[1] Read Yin's Volume III of Realm Studies. Pages 239 to 449 and appendix A

[2] Read Macrin's A Bridge to Haven; the Trail of Tears and Tribulations

[3] Read Innatala's Forgotten Path

[4] Read Soen's Research on Haven

[5] Read Ilionor's Mystics Realm

[6] Read Iai's Casual Observances and Lost Myths

Mer / Ishi-Iyai-Eyai-I

Visible indication is a blue-green liquid of a denser consistency than water.

Mer is a planet realm, a water-encased world with islands and some non-aquatic life. [1] Mer is the third planet from a hot star with higher than Earth surface temperatures and a single satellite. [2] Like Earth's humans, merfolk are the single indigenous intelligent life. Non-indigenous sentient life include the porpoises and whales, two of the numerous transplanted species between the two realms. [2]

No reported excursions into the realm have survived, and the merfolk refuse access to the realm, part of their reasoning for joining the Consociation.

Known bordering realms: Dur-Alf, Earth, and Tarus.

Interrealm travel from Earth by humans is prohibited by the Consociation Regulations. [4]

(Cont. next page; historical connection to Earth and Dur-Alf)

[1] Read Sienna's Treatise on Mer Isolation

[2] Read Tino Vangian Biography of Venis: Traitor of Mer

[6] Read Consociation Guidelines for Interrealm Treaties. Page 114.

Salmhalla

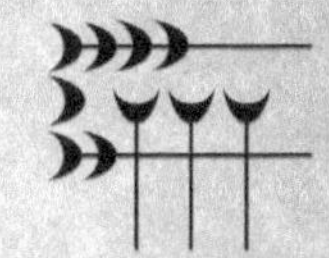

   Indications include a liquid gold which is burning hot to the touch. [1]

   Salmhalla is a plane of ambient sunlight and hot air temperatures. [1] [2] The plane contains a wide range of Earth-like terrains but predominantly includes mountains and grassy hills. [1] [2] [3] Several large water bodies have been detailed, but none rise to the level of oceans. [2] [3] [4] [5]

   Consociation guidelines prohibit interaction with the realm and dragons enforce this edict. [6]

   Known infringements have resulted in death, disappearance, mental illness, and loss of memory.

(Cont. next page; Known, theorized, and postulated magics connected to the Salmhalla realm)

[1] Read Yin's Volume IV of Realm Studies. Pages 1121 to 1349 and appendix C

[2] Read Inhai Du Anya's Scriptures of the High Dragons. Pages 89 to 97.

[3] Read Serjin's Testimonials

[4] Read Ilionor's Biography of Reshin. Pages 245 to 271.

[5] Read Wooley's Anectdotal Studies of Salmhalla

[6] Read Consociation Guidelines for Interrealm Treaties. Page 57.

Tarus

   Visible indications are a dark-gray color and a misty consistency with glittering elements akin pin head .
   Tarus is a plane realm with no ambient lighting and an oxygen-rich atmosphere. [1][2] Theories vary that the indigenous lifeforms have abilities to perceive lower frequency magnetic waves, have other senses, or solely rely on tactile and auditory senses. [2][3][4] Most grimoires record little of verifiable evidence, but specimens from the realm have been studied extensively by multiple races. [5][6] A rocky, waterless terrain is a commonly accepted description. [2][4]
   Known bordering realms: Earth, Haven, and Ya Keya.

(Cont. next page; Consociation Prohibitions)

[1] Read Yin's Volume II of Realm Studies. Pages 71 to 549 and appendix B

[2] Read Rasputin's Walks Among the Undead, the annotated version.

[3] Read Serjin's Agreements in Darkness

[4] Read Ilionor's Dedication

[5] Read Finyai's Tarus Biology

[6] Read Ted Dansworth's Research of Tarus Corporeal

Ya Keya

  Indications include a light gray mist which is moist to the touch.

  Considered the hunter's dream world, it is a plane of blue gray twilight according to numerous excursions including a Merfolk expedition led by Antre.[1] The plane contains a wide range of Earth-like terrains but predominantly includes forests, plains, and savannahs. No large water bodies have ever been detailed, but marshes and bogs were noted. [2]

  Continued interaction with the plane consistently results in a transmutation on a cellular level and the werewolf's bodily fluids become contagious. [3] Longevity and increased metabolic functions have been studied extensively. [4] [5]

  Witches and Merfolk have lost all abilities to interact with the realms once transmutation has occurred.

(Cont. next page; Known Inhabitants of Ya Keya)

[1]Read Antre's paper on *To Ya Keya: Sacrifice and Betrayal*

[2]Read Yin's *Volume III of Realm Studies*

[3]Read Jayne Dunham's *Voyage Home*

[4]Read Kizurra's *History of Akkadian Werewolves - the Dawn*

[5]Read Demot's *Monograph* for an in-depth biological reference

ACKNOWLEDGMENTS

April appears to enjoy the DRC files and has had a strong hand in helping develop some aspects. Her proofing alone has helped avoid some REALLY embarrassing mistakes.

Robyn Huss, my editor, weaves her own magic on my stories. A grammarian of the Ninth Order, she's been with me since the first series.

The Fireside Group; Siena, Rosemary, Mark, Tim, Vail, and Katharine keep me challenged to do better. Arrash and Michele from Jody Lynn Nye's DragonCon workshop keep me on task with the most intricate details and loving support. Dianne and Brett from Apex have been there for me.

I still miss David Farland's gentle mentorship. Please pick up one of his books and enjoy the magic he endowed upon the world. Writers, study his lessons at Apex Writers.

Jody Lynn Nye's workshop will always be my go to suggestion for an in-person critique for any aspiring writers. Her insight is invaluable.

Thank you.